HUNGRY LIKE HER WOLF

HUNGRY FUR LOVE
BOOK 1

C.D. GORRI

DEDICATION

To my Husband, for being my rock, and to our children for inspiring me every single day.

To Mommy, Daddy, Rina, & Missy, I miss you every single day and I know your having a great time in your Next Amazing Journey and it is as awesome as you all are.

To Tammy Payne, for keeping me in line and helping me get all my craziness straight.

To Rebecca, April, Victoria, DC, & Cara, you are my ride-or-die writing besties and I love and admire the shit out of you all.

& Last but certainly not least, to you my magical readers who joined me on this journey and are still going strong. I do it all for you.

del mare alla stella,

C.D. Gorri

HUNGRY LIKE HER WOLF
HUNGRY FUR LOVE 1 COPYRIGHT

By C.D. Gorri
Edited by BookNookNuts
Copyright © 2022, 2025

HUNGRY FUR LOVE

THE SERIES

Welcome to Castor's Corner—where the witches are curvy, the magic is unpredictable, and the fated mates come with fur, fangs, and deliciously dirty minds.

The witch trifecta of Castor's Corner is made up of three over-thirty besties who might be a magical mess, but they've got hearts of gold and zero time for nonsense—unless it comes in the form of a smoldering supernatural male.

As the guardians of their quirky, chaos-prone town, these witches are supposed to keep things under control.

Then the barrier goes down, and all magical hell breaks loose.

Now the town's crawling with trouble: ghouls in

the cemetery, talking pets with attitude, ghostly family drama, and worst of all—gorgeous shifters who might just be their fated mates.

These sexy strangers are growly, protective, and utterly devoted. And they're not backing off, no matter how messy things get.

If you love:

✔ Fated mates who can't resist a curvy witch

✔ Magical mischief and hilarious spell fails

✔ Steamy slow burns with a side of claws and cuddles

✔ Found family, fierce friendship, and paranormal chaos

Then buckle up, buttercup. The Hungry Fur Love series is here to cast a spell on your heart—and maybe your underwear.

Dive into this sizzling romcom series full of heart, heat, and happily-ever-afters with bite today!

HUNGRY LIKE HER WOLF
A CURVY WITCH MEETS GROWLY WOLF SHIFTER FATED MATES ROMANCE

One Witch. One weekend. One seriously sexy Wolf. Let the chaos begin.

Can I embrace my destiny as a Seer Witch, save my hometown, and claim my fated mate—all before Monday?

You bet my Aunt Edna–sized butt I can! Time to hike up my big girl panties and handle this supernatural s#!tstorm.

Being a Castor in Castor's Corner isn't easy. As mayor, I'm always juggling fires—sometimes literal ones. And as one-third of our Witchy Trifecta, it's my job to keep our magical town hidden from humans and protected from supernatural riffraff.

That's the plan, anyway.

Too bad I was accidentally late to our monthly coven meeting and totally forgot to renew the town's protective barrier. Oops.

Now we've got ghosts, ghouls, and smoldering-hot Shifters popping up like uninvited party guests.

The town kids are terrified of something stalking the cemetery. My besties are freaking out. And Mr.

Hottie McFurry—who may or may not be my destined mate—is stirring up all kinds of inappropriate thoughts.

Castor's Corner is going off the rails, and guess who has to fix it?

That's right. Me.

No pressure.

PROLOGUE—EVIE

A DAY in the Life of Castor's Corner Mayor Evie Castor

It was the end of another very long day, the kind of day where your pantyhose itch, your spellwork fizzles, and your familiar glares at you like you're the embarrassment to the bloodline.

So, when my phone buzzed as I waited for the world's slowest elevator, I was already one minor inconvenience away from melting into a puddle of overworked Witch goo.

Then I saw the caller ID: *The Tasty Tart.*

Only one person in the world would name their business that and proudly slap it on aprons, mugs, and tote bags. Maribella, one of my two very best friends.

The other was Donatella—stylist extraordinaire and the town's undisputed Queen of Highlights.

Together, we made up Castor's Corner's infamous Witch Trifecta. Emphasis on *tri* and *freakin' fecta*—because there were days when keeping this magical Jersey shore town together felt like holding a wet cat in a burlap sack.

I thumbed the answer button, already bracing myself.

"Evie!" Bella's voice burst through the receiver, breathless as ever.

She was always breathless. And in a rush. And probably frosting three cupcakes, scolding her sentient rolling pin, and yelling at the oven all at once.

That was just Bella. Chaos in a pastel apron. And honestly? I adored her for it.

"What's up, Bella?" I asked, trying to sound patient while aggressively stabbing the elevator button again.

The ancient lift, complete with one of those clanky accordion gates, sat there like it was on a coffee break.

Castor's Corner City Hall was as old as the town itself. Possibly older.

The place had charm, sure, if by charm you

meant crumbling bricks, haunted bathrooms, and an elevator that moved slower than molasses in a blizzard.

Magic didn't work inside municipal buildings—*something about too many wards and not enough funding*—so I couldn't even zap the stupid thing into motion.

And trust me, I'd tried.

Repeatedly.

Possibly while hangry.

"Evie, are you even listening?" Bella chirped, snapping me out of my elevator-induced rage spiral.

"Trying," I muttered, blowing out a breath and shifting the phone to my other ear. "Hard to concentrate when this death trap is giving me side-eye."

Bella launched into one of her signature rambles. Something about burned lemon tarts, a mysteriously vanishing bag of flour, and a flirtatious customer who kept lingering by the bakery case like he was definitely not trying to get some free cookies.

Typical day in Castor's Corner.

I closed my eyes and leaned against the cool stone wall, letting her voice wash over me like sugar-laced static.

I loved Bella.

I loved Donny.

I even loved this insane little town where Witches, Shifters, and Ghosts all played house like we were on some cursed reality show.

But I was so. Damn. Tired.

Being the mayor of a supernatural town wasn't all ribbon cuttings and parade floats.

It was damage control, diplomacy, and trying not to strangle your constituents when they insisted the library ghost was stealing their cardigans again.

And now? With the protective barrier needing reaffirming and me running late, I was feeling the pressure.

I mean, no mayor in the *history* of Castor's Corner had ever missed a ward-strengthening night. Not once. And I knew better. I *knew* I couldn't afford to slip—not with all the magical chaos bubbling just beneath our charming, pastel-painted surface.

Heck, the whole town couldn't afford it.

But sure. Let's talk about cupcakes. Priorities, right?

I tuned back just in time to hear Bella wail, "—and then the frosting exploded, Evie. Exploded. Do you know what pink buttercream does to a cashmere blend?"

I didn't. But I had a feeling I was about to find

out, possibly with photographic evidence and a rant about designer dry cleaning costs.

The elevator finally groaned to life with a wheeze and a thunk, like it too had given up on the day. As I stepped inside, gripping my phone and the last thread of my sanity, one thought spun through my frosting-deprived, mildly frizzed brain.

This town is going to eat me alive if I don't figure things out—and fast.

Preferably before the full moon.

Or before my Witch Trifecta accidentally broke the supernatural world. Again.

Either way, the writing was on the wall. *And in my planner. And probably scrawled in magical ink across the town's ley lines.*

In fact, I was sure of it.

I mean, here I was—thirty-something, single, slightly magical, and one more stressor away from turning into a feral raccoon in yoga pants.

My hair was frizzing from emotional instability and humidity, my under-eye bags had their own zip code, and don't even get me started on my to-do list.

The font on that scroll of doom had shrunk three times just to fit the page.

What did a Witch have to do to get a little R&R, for fuck's sake?

A weekend with no crises, no potluck-turned-portal events, no spontaneous hauntings in aisle five at Hex-Mart.

Was that so much to ask?

Apparently, yes. Yes, it was.

Because instead of a massage and a mimosa, I was stuck managing magical infrastructure, trying to keep our town from imploding, and dodging enchanted baked goods like they were grenades with frosting.

And don't even get me started on the love life I didn't have.

Where was my tall, growly, emotionally constipated fated mate? Huh?

Did I miss my cue?

Was he stuck in traffic?

Probably.

Knowing my luck, he was circling the town square trying to parallel park and questioning his entire life.

So yeah.

Things were unraveling, I was spiraling, and I had a bad feeling about the upcoming full moon bonfire.

It felt like life was about to get a lot more complicated than the usual chanting, spark showers, and fireproof panties.

And yet? I couldn't shake the tiniest flutter in my chest.

Because deep down, in the weird, glitter-glazed center of my chaotic Witch heart, I had a feeling that something big was coming.

Something wild.

Something dangerous.

Something delicious.

Gaia help me, I wasn't sure if I was ready.

Little did I know, ready or not, Castor's Corner was about to get a whole lot messier.

And so was I.

"Evie, did you even hear what I said about the spell?" Bella snapped.

"Sorry, Bella, you're cutting out," I lied, with all the conviction of a woman who'd used that excuse daily since the invention of cell phones.

"Oh, hush up. I know you better than you think." She wasn't wrong. "Anyway, listen—I think I might have finally cracked the spell! You know, *the* spell to take the calories out of my Double Devil's Food Delights!"

Just hearing the name made my mouth water.

Bella's baking wasn't just good—*it was dangerous.*

Her pastries had started more fights than the

high school football team's last three losing seasons combined.

One time, right before Easter, she'd made a batch of Chocolate Bunny Supreme cupcakes.

They sold out in under twelve minutes and sparked a literal fistfight in front of her shop window.

The sheriff had to intervene. And by the sheriff, I mean both the sheriff and his only deputy—poor old Charles, a Sloth Shifter who unfortunately did not have the heart for high-speed cupcake riots.

The funeral had been a quiet, somber affair.

Bella provided coffee and muffins afterward. They were lemon poppy seed muffins. And they were divine, which felt wildly inappropriate and also exactly right.

So yeah, when she said she was working on a spell to make her baked goods guilt-free?

Sign. Me. Up.

"All I have to do," she continued, voice practically fizzing with excitement, "is enchant the batter at precisely 425 degrees while reciting the incantation à la mode—*that's the name I gave it, cute right?*—and boom! Same rich flavor, zero magical weight retention!"

It was charming how optimistic she sounded.

Dangerous, but charming.

While she babbled on about sugar stabilization and calorie sigils, my brain wandered. Because that's what it does when I'm faced with pseudoscience, Witchcraft and pastry-based miracles.

I was reminded of something Magdalena, the next La Befana, had once told me on a Swoosh call.

For the record, Swoosh is the magical world's answer to Zoom, except we don't glitch, freeze, or spontaneously combust from spell interference.

Usually.

The app was created by a group of techno-mancers—*Witches and Wizards who cast using technology as focal points instead of your average magic wand*—who got fed up with blown routers and melting phones.

Honestly, bless them.

Anyway, during one of our mandatory leadership check-ins, Magdalena—*La Befana*, the curly, redheaded terror of the east coast coven circuit, second only to Sherry Morgan-McAllister, aka *The Morrigan* (capital *T*, capital *M*)—once gave me a nugget of profound magical wisdom.

"The point of something being so damn good is that there's always a cost."

She hadn't been talking about money.

Gaia, no.

In this case, she meant love handles.

Because nothing in life, not even a magically enchanted, zero-calorie chocolate cupcake with a ganache swirl and edible glitter dust, comes free.

Magic had rules.

Unfortunately, so did hips.

And in my case? Both were beginning to feel cursed.

But that was the cost of Maribella's killer Double Devil's Food Delights.

Those bite-sized chocolate cake-cookie hybrids —*stuffed with homemade buttercream and whatever sinful filling she'd concocted that week*—were what dreams and waistband regret were made of.

I wasn't exaggerating when I said people had been maimed trying to get their hands on them during Sunday brunch or holiday pre-orders.

Another time, her bakery got a write-up in the Castor's Corner Chronicle calling it "more dangerous than an ogre biker bar."

That gem came after last year's Samhain Festival, when two Big Cat Shifters threw down—*literally clawed each other's clothes off*—over the last Peanut Butter Delight.

It ended with one in the ER, one in jail, and Bella

crying because someone crushed the cupcake during the fight.

"Sounds great, Bella," I said, doing my best to sound supportive and not like I was silently reliving the trauma of her last magical baking experiment.

"It is, right?" she beamed through the phone.

"But how do you know it worked?" I asked, instantly suspicious.

The kind of suspicion that had you sniffing your drink at brunch because you just knew someone slipped a truth serum in it for funsies.

See, being a Witch came with rules. One of the big ones? You don't use magic for your own personal gain.

It's like *Witchcraft 101*.

Break that rule and the universe has a tendency to slap your face with irony—*or slime.*

Maribella knew that. It's why she never tested her enchanted goods on herself.

Fool me once, I thought grimly.

"Well, um, I don't, Evie Love," she admitted sheepishly. "Not for sure. That's why I wanted you to try them out."

She whispered that last part like I wouldn't notice.

"Uh uh. No way," I said immediately, already tasting doom.

Or worse—*salty sludge masquerading as chocolate.*

"Come on! I'll bring them to the field tonight, after we finish recharging the wards," she said in that singsong voice she used when bribing us with sugar.

"Bella, I will not be your guinea pig," I warned, stern and unflinching.

Not again. Not after The Incident.

Last time she asked me to "just taste this real quick," I ended up with a mouth full of what I can only describe as cursed pudding.

Slimy. Bitter. Lumpy.

I'd gagged so hard I saw the veil.

Even now, my overactive gag reflex was threatening to rise like an angry sea god.

Gaia, take me now.

"Ohmygawd! Evie, stop exaggerating," Bella growled, clearly offended by my totally justified food trauma.

"Not. Sorry. Gotta—" I clutched my stomach as another dry heave threatened to bubble up.

The memory was too fresh.

Too moist.

It took a few deep breaths and some mental shielding to calm down.

The taste might be gone, but the betrayal lingered.

Look, I knew Magdelena was right when she said everything has a price. I mean, La Befana was typically right about most things.

In this case, she wasn't talking about money. She meant consequence.

Balance.

That's magic, baby.

The bummer, though?

Witch metabolism was supposed to be off the charts.

Fast, efficient, the kind of thing that lets you devour a cinnamon roll and still zip your jeans.

But somehow, my besties and I had gotten the short end of the supernatural stick.

Maybe it was our Italian genes.

Maybe it was the carbs.

Or maybe it was the universe being petty.

Whatever the reason, Bella, Donny, and I were not your typical sleek and svelte Witches.

We were curvy.

Soft.

Sturdy.

Hungry.

But not just for cookies and cupcakes and salted caramel spells.

We were hungry for more.

For laughter that felt like home.

For partners who didn't just tolerate the magic and the madness, but relished it.

For hands that didn't flinch at hips or thighs or bellies but gripped them with reverence.

We wanted it all.

The cake, the coven, and the kind of love that felt like magic.

And maybe, just maybe, if we didn't completely wreck the wards tonight, the universe might finally throw us a bone.

Or some sexy as all get men made just for us.

Preferably the kind with a jawline that could cut glass and a growl that curled toes.

Yes, please.

CHAPTER ONE-EVIE

LATER THAT SAME **Day**

After I left City Hall—*finally freed from that creaky, bureaucratic crypt*—I headed out to run a quick errand before meeting the Witch Trifecta at our usual ritual spot.

Just your average pre-bonfire pit stop.

No biggie.

My mind was buzzing louder than an entire Gremlin Hive on Red Bull.

Bella's "maybe safe" calorie-reduction spell was still fresh on my mental playlist. My stomach, ever the opportunist, took that as an invitation to growl loud enough to scare a passing raccoon.

Then there was the firefighter shortage. We had

exactly two on staff—*one of whom was more flammable than helpful.*

Not great when your town's top three annual events involve open flames, enchanted fireworks, or rogue pyromancers.

Sheriff Davies had also hinted—*again*—that he was ready to retire and *"finally spend some quality time ice fishing with Myrtle,"* which was code for sit on his porch and complain about politics to his wife until she hexes him into a mute spell.

And of course, the eternal curse of Castor's Corner. The parking situation.

Sigh. Deep, soul-weary, exhausted-Witch sigh.

Looking back now, maybe that was why the spell went sideways.

Or maybe it was because Donatella decided—on ritual night, no less—to bleach her midnight-black hair and go for teal with attitude.

The only thing that color had was regret.

Or perhaps it was Maribella's fault.

She scorched the caramel filling for her dulce de leche doughnuts and refused to accept defeat, choosing instead to *charm the bitterness out.*

That poor doughnut ended up tasting like heartbreak and burned toast.

Any one of those things could've nudged the universe out of alignment.

Or maybe the stars were already misaligned.

Mercury was retrograde.

Or maybe fate just decided to fuck with us just for shits and giggles.

Whatever the reason, what should've been our usual full moon bonfire and standard-issue ward-strengthening spell turned into a clusterfuck of epic, spark-spitting, ley line-rattling proportions.

To summarize, we fucked up.

Big time.

And that's how I found myself in the middle of my woods—post-spell, slightly singed, naked as the day I was born, and blinking at the sight of three tall, muscle-bound, sex-on-a-stick strangers standing in a patch of glowing ash like they'd just fallen out of a fantasy calendar.

They were definitely Shifters.

You could tell by the eyes.

And the aura.

And the fact that they smelled like fresh pine, testosterone, and bad decisions.

Their monster-sized SUV sat dead right behind them, somehow not even dusty despite the mud and dirt on the road.

Country music played low from the cracked-open windows, the twangy drawl clashing violently with my mounting rage.

One of them had the audacity to smile at me.

Fucking smile—can you believe that?

"Excuse me, the name's Jaxson," he said, all Southern charm and sinful biceps, "and I was wonderin' if you could help us? Is this Maccon City?"

I blinked.

Twice.

Then I channeled every drop of righteous fury passed down to me from generations of strong Castor women and snapped.

"No. This is not Maccon City. You're in Castor's Corner. I'm Evelyn Castor—mayor and pissed-off citizen—and unless one of you brought a fire extinguisher, a peace offering, or a damn portal key to reverse a magical disaster, I suggest you stop smiling and start explaining."

And this moment right there? This was the moment everything changed.

And me? I hadn't even had a doughnut yet.

So, how did everything go wrong? Well. Let's start at the beginning.

CHAPTER TWO–EVIE

EARLIER THAT SAME **Day**

It all started when my car blew a gasket.

Or tore a belt.

Or snapped a mana-link cable.

Honestly, I had no idea what actually went wrong—some kind of garage-speak nonsense that made my eyes glaze over and my brain tap out.

All I knew was the engine hiccupped, coughed like a dying dragon, and gave up the ghost.

Suffice it to say my car glitched.

I was late for work at the start of the day, and everything went downhill from there.

Which was a shame, really. Because it was Thursday, and Thursdays were supposed to be my pre-weekend happy place.

I'd been looking forward to two blissful days of taste-testing Maribella's newest bakery experiments —*possibly featuring cursed cronuts*—and getting a mani-pedi from Donny, who'd just received her latest shipment of enchanted nail polish.

I'd had my eye on a color called *Purple Rain,* allegedly inspired by La Befana herself.

According to Donny, the glittery concoction would turn your nails into reflective disco balls— *mirror magic with extra sass.*

I wanted it purely for the entertainment value.

Couldn't hurt to blind a few political adversaries with fabulous fingertips.

Yeah, okay, it was a little dorky.

But what could I say? I was a sucker for shiny things and supernatural glam.

Anyway, I should have known it was all going to hell when my coffee maker belched out thick black sludge instead of my premium French roast.

The smell alone could have raised the dead— and not in a good, "Yay! Grandpa's back!" kind of way.

By the time the truck gave out—*again*—I was already halfway to a meltdown.

That made three breakdowns this month alone.

And before you say it, yes, I know I should've

replaced it years ago. But this wasn't just any clunker.

It was my grandmother's red Chevy pickup, handed down with pride and powered by spite and nostalgia.

She named it *Lucia* after her favorite opera singer and swore it was sturdy enough to outrun a Hellhound in heat.

I was emotionally attached, irrationally loyal, and maybe just a teensy bit cursed.

It was all I had left of her, aside from the house I grew up in and my long, straight, undeniably Roman nose.

Whatever. The nose gave me character. *And* it made me look distinguished, I decided when I was in college, especially when paired with the right lipstick.

See, I tried a magical nose job once when I was sixteen and insecure.

Huge mistake.

My nose had grown an extra inch and a half overnight, curving slightly to the left like a cursed parsnip.

Nonna, bless her twisted little heart, made me walk around like that for twenty-four hours as a punishment for magical vanity.

"Let this be a lesson," she'd said, cackling and sipping espresso as I cried over a hand mirror. *"Next time, use contour."*

Needless to say, I never attempted magical plastic surgery again.

Some lessons get etched right into your trauma.

Now standing beside my stubborn, broken-down truck on the side of Witchwood Lane, I sighed, pulled out my cell, and dialed the only person who knew how to coax Lucia back to life.

"Auto Boys! We work your body right!" came the gravelly shout of Jeffrey Hardwick, town mechanic and professional menace to HR departments everywhere.

"Jeffrey," I said, deadpan. "How many times do I have to tell you that slogan's gonna get you sued?"

"Hasn't happened yet, Madam Mayor," he said, laughing like a coyote in a cornfield. "And I ain't changing it. It's memorable."

Jeff was older than sin, half Gremlin on his mother's side, and ran the only garage in town.

The man looked like he'd rolled out of a toolbox in 1972 and just kept going, fueled by motor oil and mischief.

But despite the outdated catchphrases and tragic

comb-over, the guy knew cars. And he treated Lucia with something like respect.

"Truck's down again," I told him. "It's making that sputtering cough and then just dies. Like a dramatic Victorian heroine, but less poetic."

"Again? Evie," he groaned. "When are you gonna give up on that hunk of junk and get yourself something made in this century? Something with actual brakes and airbags that don't smell like mothballs?"

"What would you do for work if I did?" I countered.

That shut him up for a second.

"Fine," he grumbled. "I'll send Mikey to grab it."

Ah, Mikey. The long-suffering son. Lived at home. Probably played way too much *Dungeons & Demons* as a kid.

He once tried to flirt with me at the Founder's Day dance by comparing my eyes to ancient magical mud pies.

Sweet kid. But too skinny.

He wouldn't survive five minutes with me.

"You know," Jeffrey added with a little too much casual cheer, "Mikey did mention how nice you looked the other day."

"Forget it, Jeffrey," I said sharply.

"Oh, come on now—"

"Goodbye, Jeffrey."

I hung up and ordered a WUber—*our town's magical ride-share service.*

It was like Uber, but with cars, trucks, sometimes broomsticks and questionable drinks and snacks.

As I waited, I took a deep breath, glared at the broken truck, and tried to tell myself this was just a minor hiccup in a totally manageable day.

But deep down, I knew the truth.

The day was simply cursed.

I just didn't know my truck acting up was the beginning of everything going wrong.

As for Mikey, let's just say dating an iron-wielding half-Gremlin was not on my *to do* list.

Don't look at me like that.

I'm not *speciesist.*

I already said the guy was half my size. I'm way too curvy for the likes of Mikey.

But since you asked, *yes*, interspecies mixing did occur in the supernatural world, but I had to acknowledge it could result in some strange ass looking children.

Take my cousin Waldo.

The man had yellow-tinted skin that made it almost impossible to pass in the normal world.

Lucky for him, he could always claim he had liver disease to account for the yolkish tint.

Everyone in Castor's Corner was at least part supernatural.

As such, they were aware of the rules of our world, and keeping it secret was of the utmost importance.

That's where the Witch Trifecta comes in.

See, I'm one of the three Witches chosen to guard our town from outsiders.

Especially non-magical ones.

My name is Evelyn Castor, fondly called Evie, or even little Evie, by the townsfolk.

Yes, I am a descendant of the town's forebears.

I'm also a certified magical Witch, with a cache of powers I inherited from my ancestors, and my special gift is *the sight*.

That's right, I can sometimes get peeks into the future, and occasionally, I can even see and chat with the *dearly departed*.

But on this particular Thursday, I was totally and completely *blind*.

I had a huge, dark, bulbous clusterfuck of a cloud system portending all kinds of doom and gloom hanging over my head.

I just couldn't see it.

And as I waited for my WUber, I had literally no idea all hell was going to break loose later that night.

"Hey Evie, get in!" A much welcomed, and noticeably absent of late, voice boomed from a few feet away.

I stilled a moment before replying and grabbed my phone.

Looking down at the open WUber app for supernatural transport within city limits, I saw that Stanley was listed as my driver.

The app pinged, and I looked down to see he had marked himself as *arrived* and *client retrieved*.

Another ping sounded, and I frowned as I read.

The fucker gave himself a 30% tip, probably using my login.

He had set it up, after all.

Stanley knew all my secrets.

Well, most of them.

As my fabulous former administrative assistant, he sorta set up all my accounts and knew all my passwords.

Kind of made his leaving a huge pain in my round ass.

Especially when I wanted to update my supernatural social media and *Date to Mate* accounts.

Date to Mate was like a magical dating app created

by Uncle Uzzi, the magical matchmaker extraordinaire himself.

There was also Windr, which was more like a hookup app for supes, *Witches in particular.*

Those just looking to get down and dirty without strings.

I happened to have a healthy attitude about sex, even if I never used the thing, I wanted to keep my options open.

Okay, fine, Stanley downloaded the app without my permission and set up an account for me.

He thought I needed to get laid because of the high stress levels of my job.

Did I mention I was the mayor?

Yeah, I did.

Okay, well, anyway, I was shocked to see him in front of me.

What the eye of newt was he doing here?

"You're driving for WUber?" I asked, shaking my head as I got into his super clean and brand spanking new BMW.

"I have to. It's not like you pay me enough," he said, winking and handing me a cup of steaming hot coffee and a cruller from Maribella's bakery.

"Am I paying you at all anymore? I thought you ran away to follow your cock, I mean *heart* to greener pastures," I said, taking the goodies before he could pull them back.

"Evelyn Castor!" Stanley yelled my name in mock outrage.

I knew he wasn't really angry.

The Wizard was bawdier than anyone else I knew.

Thank Gaia, he found a man to fully appreciate that side of him. Otherwise, I'd have to take the fucker out.

Stanley was a close friend of mine. He wasn't one of the Trifecta, but he was next in line as one of my besties.

"You know, it boggles the mind why I'd even consider working for you," he snarked. "Alas, Stephen has his job, and though I am too good for you, no one else can fill this position the way I can."

"That's what Stephen said," I replied snarkily.

Well, as snarkily as I could manage with a mouth full of cruller.

Truth was, I was relieved as fuck.

When Stanley and Stephen got married last spring, I was devastated to lose my assistant.

The man had a superior talent for cutting through red tape and getting the city council to back the fuck down. When he announced his impending marriage and told me he was leaving—*quite suddenly, mind you*—I did the only thing I could.

I cried and pleaded and begged.

But the course of true love had run amok all over my fucking life. Like it had been since I hit puberty.

And this was all about the same time my relationship took a big fat crap on me, also known as *my boyfriend dumped me*, stating I was too demanding and had no time for him.

Losing my ex was nothing compared to losing Stanley.

Love truly sucked balls as far as I was concerned.

It never worked out for me.

And to add insult to injury, love went and took the only person I could ever fathom working with for any amount of time—*oh hell no!*

Okay, fine.

I had a teeny-tiny people problem.

See, I hate them. People. All of them.

As for love?

Yeah, um, well, to hell with that shit.

I had no use for that starry-eyed, chest-aching, stomach-flipping nonsense.

Just thinking about it made me itchy.

Like, full-blown break-out-in-hives, hand-me-the-calamine kind of itchy.

And no, it wasn't because I'd grown up unloved. Quite the opposite. I came from a big, loud, affectionate family full of spell-slingers, sauce-stirrers, and unsolicited advice-givers.

I knew what love could look like.

I just also knew what it looked like when it turned sour.

Because some of my relatives—bless their spell-bound hearts—had a real problem keeping that love in the family.

And I don't mean in a creepy cousin way.

I mean committing to the damn thing.

Nonna had loved Grandpa Al with everything she had.

Like epic romance, write-a-novel-about-it level love. And then? He skipped town.

Disappeared into the mist—*or, more accurately, the Pine Barrens*—with barely a note and a promise to *find himself*.

Newsflash: he didn't find himself.

Unless *yourself* is code for twenty years of zero contact and ghosting the entire family before literally ghosting.

Nonna mourned the old bastard till her dying day.

Never looked at another man.

Never wanted to.

That kind of grief? That changes a girl.

It leaves residue. Sticky emotional goo that clings to your soul and whispers, *Don't you dare fall in love. You'll end up stirring soup for one and crying into your cannoli.*

So yeah. Love had a lousy rep, at least from where I was standing.

But enough of that. Back to Stanley.

"Okay, your honeymoon was sooooo long," I drawled dramatically, flopping back into the seat of his glam-as-hell car. "Now spill. I want details. How was Europe?"

"Old. Gloomy. Overpriced," he said with a dismissive wave. "I missed me some good old Jersey Shore sunshine and overpriced cotton candy."

Then he gunned the engine and made a sharp U-turn across a double yellow line.

"That's illegal, you maniac," I hissed.

"It's fine. I know people," he replied with a wink.

God, I'd missed him.

I didn't want to say it out loud—*not yet*—but seeing him again made me feel like I could breathe.

Being mayor of a supernatural town was like running daycare for magical creatures with access to alcohol and explosives.

And since my name was literally Castor, people expected me to sacrifice every part of myself for the town's wellbeing.

And I did. I do.

But some days, it felt like no one saw me.

Except for Donatella. And Maribella. And Stanley.

Stanley, who was equal parts admin assistant, sass-fueled life coach, and emergency wine supplier.

He was the rare soul who'd tell me I was being ridiculous and re-alphabetize my potion files while I sulked about it.

He was also the only person on Earth who could call me out with flair and Gucci.

I studied him, bracing myself for the news I didn't want to hear. That this was just a quick visit.

That he and Stephen were flying off to some moonlit beach where the champagne sparkled and the air didn't smell like salt, bonfires, and slightly burned magic.

I couldn't handle losing him again. Not when I'd only just started pretending, I was okay without him.

Stanley looked over, pushing his sunglasses up into his hair. "Alright, young lady. I know exactly what's going on in that Witchy little head of yours."

Note to self: steal those shades the second he leaves them unattended.

"I don't know what you're talking about," I sniffed, prim and defensive.

"Sure you don't. Which is why I'm just going to say it—*dramatically, of course.*"

He took a deep, showy inhale like he was about to belt out a Broadway number.

"After a luxurious three-month honeymoon across Europe—during which I was adored, pampered, and stuffed with sinful cheeses—Stephen and I have decided to move home. To Castor's Corner. Permanently."

I blinked. My heart stuttered.

I wanted to play it cool. Truly. But I lasted all of two seconds before squealing and bouncing like a caffeinated pixie on his plush leather seat.

"Really? Like really *really*? You. Here. Back home. For good?!"

Stanley grinned. "OMG, yes, Evie. Holy Gaia, you reek of desperation."

I gasped, scandalized. "How dare you."

But I was glowing. I could feel it.

The tension in my chest cracked open like a bad spell jar, and all that hope and joy came pouring out.

I'd missed him so much it actually hurt.

He reached over and gave me a quick hug. The kind that was brief but grounding—warm arms, lavender-scented cologne, the hum of Wizard magic crackling like champagne bubbles around us.

I was so moved I nearly dropped my doughnut.

Nearly. Let's not be dramatic.

"Stephen knows how I feel about this place, cupcake," Stanley said softly. "He gets it. So, we're staying. And we just hired a contractor to restore the old Gardner mansion. Between helping you run this town and rebuilding that creaky palace, I'll be plenty busy. And when Stephen's off kicking ass on Wall Street, I'll be holding down the supernatural fort."

His magic danced around the interior of the car in twinkling shades of lilac and silver, dusting the air with sparkle and peace.

That was Stanley's magic—*always a little fabulous, always a little fierce, and always just what I needed.*

We'd been inseparable since preschool—back when friendship meant snack swaps, secret pinkie pacts, and a shared obsession with sparkle.

Stanley had asked to try on my pink plastic princess heels during dress-up time, and I'd said, "You better slay if you wanna rock them."

He *did.*

And honestly? He's been slaying ever since.

My mother, of course, had a fit every time I wore those heels, certain I was one step away from snapping my ankle like a dry wishbone.

She wasn't wrong.

To this day, I still couldn't walk in anything higher than an inch without risking my dignity and skeletal alignment.

Stanley, on the other hand? The man could sprint in stilettos. *Backwards.*

So yes, I was now a flats-only kind of Witch—and that was just too damn bad for any tall guys I dated.

I'd already sacrificed one prom night and a week of mobility to the evil gods of platform heels.

Never again.

Some things were simply *not* worth the pain.

Like high heels.

Or Wizards named Richard.

But I digress.

"Hmm, nice loafers," Stanley remarked, giving me an approving once-over.

"Thank you," I replied with a humble nod, as if I didn't spend forty-five minutes picking these out this morning.

They were my favorite pair. Aquamarine-dyed

vegan leather with tiny magenta tassels, gold beading, and teal rubber soles.

Magical, comfortable, and obnoxiously cute—*like me.*

Stanley, for his part, was decked out in at least four different shades of purple—including a silky lavender button-down and eggplant slacks so sharply creased they could cut through dimensions.

The man was a peacock and proud of it.

"Did the city council finally revoke that idiot's permit to move the fire hydrants?" he asked casually, like we weren't still recovering from that magical traffic nightmare.

"Yes and no," I said with a sigh. "I've been sneaking around at night putting them back one by one."

Our *former* fire chief—*bless his aggressively useless heart*—had gotten the brilliant idea to *optimize response times* by shifting all the hydrants six inches into the street.

All he did was create a hydra-headed hydra of parking tickets, fender benders, and angry citizens threatening to sue the town.

Stanley rolled his eyes. "Idiots."

The city council was mostly made up of Wizards, so yes—*idiots* was accurate.

Not that Stanley was a traitor to his own kind.

He just had *eyes.*

And common sense.

Honestly, he was more Witch than Wizard, anyway.

The whole penis thing was just a technicality.

We chatted as we climbed the stairs to my office, coffee in one hand, fried carb deliciousness in the other.

I was basking in the warmth of having Stanley back.

One of my best friends, my sass backup, my scheduling savior.

And now that he was here, it actually felt like I had a shot at surviving this week with my soul intact.

His husband Stephen was a gem, too. A half-Goblin financier who managed hedge funds like a battlefield general.

He adored Stanley, respected his magic, and had once threatened to sue a hotel into oblivion for overcharging us on a coven retreat.

My kind of guy.

"So, did I mention I just hired a contractor to redo our new place?" Stanley said, practically vibrating with joy. "I still can't believe we're moving into the old Gardner mansion. I mean, I've *always* known I was meant to be the lord of a manor."

I snorted. "Please. You've been playing that role since preschool. All you're missing is a butler and a wine cellar full of mood lighting."

"All I'm saying is," he went on, striking a dramatic pose, "after work, I plan to greet my very busy, *very* sexy husband—fresh from conquering Wall Street—in a silk robe and velvet slippers, cocktail in hand. Maybe even a monocle. Haven't decided yet."

A shimmer of lilac-hued Wizard magic burst around him like glittery confetti, all sparkle and smug satisfaction.

"Okay, TMI, pal," I laughed, pretending to gag but secretly soaking up every second.

And yeah, maybe there was a teeny-tiny flash of envy—*gone as fast as it came.*

I wasn't proud.

But truth? I felt lighter just being near him.

We reached my office, coffees in hand, spirits high.

Finally. A good moment.

"I was thinking," Stanley said, flipping open his enchanted tablet. "We tackle the new rec area permits first, then review the fire chief applicants—

Oh my Gaia, Evie, do we *still* not have anyone to replace Daniels and his crew?"

"Still vacant," I muttered.

It had been a hundred years since the great fire that decimated half of Castor's Corner, and we still hadn't found a permanent fire crew willing to stay.

We had volunteers, sure, but no one wanted the job full time. Not since the last squad mysteriously aged thirty years after one too many magical flare-ups.

And let's not even talk about the sheriff. The man was ready to retire and had already started crocheting in his office.

I was one emergency away from appointing a talking raven as interim law enforcement.

"Yeah, well," I sighed, "Daniels wasn't right for the job, anyway."

Or for me.

Stanley glanced at me but didn't comment. Bless him. He *could have.*

I knew he wanted to say something about my tragically bad taste in men.

Especially Richard "Dick" Daniels—*the Wizard ex-fire chief with all the charm of a tax audit.*

Stanley simply cleared his throat and said, "So, what shall we tackle first, Madam Mayor?"

His chipper tone yanked me out of my pit of regret. I opened my mouth to answer—*and that's when the yelling started.*

A chorus of voices exploded from the lobby like a banshee chorus in a blender.

"Madam Mayor!"

"Evie!"

"I am still waiting on my appeal!"

"You said you'd hex my neighbor's squirrel infestation!"

I turned the corner to see a dozen angry towns-folk crowding the lobby, shaking scrolls and peti-tions and—*was that a floating ferret with glowing eyes?*

"Holy shitballs, Evie!" Stanley hissed. "What the *eff* went on here while I was gone?"

He immediately launched into assistant mode, waving his hands and tossing out calming spells like candy.

I slammed my office door shut behind me and slid to the floor, muffin crumbs on my skirt and doom in my heart.

It was Thursday.

But make no mistake.

It was the Mondayest Thursday ever.

And I had a bad, bad feeling it was only going to get worse.

CHAPTER THREE—EVIE

"What are you saying, Miss Spritely?" I asked, doing my best not to sigh audibly as the town's most dramatic elementary school principal cornered me two steps from freedom.

Stanley, already halfway out the door, gave me a sympathetic wave and tapped his watch with exaggerated flair.

The universal wrap it up, woman gesture.

I shot him a helpless look as Miss Spritely's voice rose another octave, drilling directly into my brain like a caffeinated Banshee.

It was officially after office hours. I was supposed to be heading to the woods to meet the Witch Trifecta for our monthly ward-strengthening ritual.

You know, the one that kept our town from being overrun with chaos and creatures from beyond?

But noooo. I was stuck here, dealing with a hysterical principal on the edge of a full magical meltdown.

"Are you not concerned about our children at all, Madam Mayor?" she shrieked directly into my ear like I had just endorsed demon-led daycare.

I winced. My head throbbed in perfect rhythm with every step I took toward the elevator, praying it would open quickly so I could escape to the sweet, sweet embrace of fresh air and Witchy bonfires.

"Of course, I want our kids to be safe," I said, summoning every ounce of calm and professionalism I had left—*which, to be fair, was running dangerously low.* "But maybe you could—not scream at me while I try to help?"

I could practically hear how my bestie Donatella would have reacted to this whole thing. She was probably snorting from afar even now.

Donny would've zapped this woman into silence in under five seconds.

Maribella would've nodded empathetically while plotting her death via poisoned caramel glaze.

Me? I was the mayor.

The elected adult in the room.

Which meant I had to smile, nod, and absorb verbal abuse like a human sponge with a taxpayer-funded salary.

As my Nonna always said, *"Politics is a tightrope walk, bambina. And sometimes, you gotta do it in heels with a Werewolf biting at your ankles."*

Sage advice.

"I'll notify the sheriff about the incident," I said, attempting reason. "But how exactly can I help you right now, Miss Spritely?"

I held out a sliver of hope that she might say thank you and hang up.

Ha. No such luck.

Instead, she launched into a detailed list of student names, ages, and tardy times down to the minute.

Which wouldn't be quite so ridiculous if we didn't already have a dedicated truancy officer for this exact kind of thing.

Emily Borzi, our feline Shifter truancy officer extraordinaire, had apparently taken the complaint earlier today.

But instead of handling Miss Spritely's concerns herself, Officer Borzi directed the high-strung principal straight to me.

Smart kitty.

I made a mental note to have a very stern chat with Emily—*and possibly lure her into compliance with a new scratching post and some smoked salmon.*

"I still don't understand why you're calling me," I said, somehow still calm. Mostly. Barely. "I'm the mayor, not the magical school crossing guard."

"Because, Evie Castor, it is your job to ensure the safety of this town," she snapped, using my full name like she was about to assign me detention.

"There's something going on at the Castor's Corner Cemetery. Something unnatural. Something that's scaring our children. It's your duty to investigate and expel that unsettled spirit before it attracts attention we don't want."

And just like that, she hung up with a theatrical huff worthy of a soap opera villain.

"Shit," I muttered, staring at my phone like it had personally betrayed me.

I jabbed the screen to hang up—*too late*—and bit my lip hard enough to leave a dent in my soul.

My thoughts swirled into a frenzy.

Ghosts in the cemetery? Now?

Was someone pulling a prank?

Or was there really something lurking among the headstones, creeping out magical kids before homeroom?

Let's not forget that Castor's Corner had quite the reputation for magical schooling.

We even had our own magical university, *the Royal Academy for Magical Advancement*, which was something like if Hogwarts started in junior high and went all the way through college.

It brought in a ton of money and support from the supernatural world. Point was, we couldn't afford to have any damage done to our schooling rep. And that, of course, started with Miss Spritely's kids.

My phone let out a sudden high-pitched beep, then flashed an ominous shade of green before going completely black.

I blinked.

Then, I seriously considered hurling the damn thing at the nearest wall.

Because this? This was not how my Thursday night was supposed to go.

Witches and technology were kind of at war. Not like full-on fireballs and EMPs (though, let's be real, we'd definitely win), but more like a long-standing cold war full of glitches, sparks, and mutual contempt.

Magic and microchips just didn't mix. You cast a spell near a Wi-Fi router, and poof—suddenly every device in a three-block radius is streaming goat yoga from 2009 and no one can explain why.

But recently, I'd discovered a few glorious exceptions to the rule.

Enter: Swoosh, WUber, Date to Mate, and a whole suite of magical apps designed for modern Witches with lives to run and curses to manage.

After jumping through enough bureaucratic hoops to make the DMV look like a dream vacation, I'd been granted a special magical license to operate my cell phone legally within Castor's Corner.

That meant hexing via phone? Totally possible.

Ordering potion ingredients on-demand? Yep.

Need a spell kit delivered to your doorstep in thirty minutes or less? There's an app for that.

It made 21st-century life a little easier for us supes and helped us blend in when we ventured beyond our magically camouflaged borders.

No more pulling out dusty tomes in Starbucks or explaining why your "Uber" was actually a broomstick named Dolores.

Finally, after coaxing, cursing, and threatening bodily harm, I got my phone to turn back on.

Just in time for the alarm I'd set to buzz like an angry hornet in my palm.

"Crap," I muttered, frowning hard enough to give myself premature forehead lines.

I was officially late.

Again.

I slung my purse over my shoulder like a warrior preparing for battle and launched my voice-to-text app to jot down a few notes about Miss Spritely's ghosty freak-out.

Unfortunately, the damn thing still hated my Jersey Shore accent with a fiery passion.

"Note: *Cast of honor ghost* in—ugh. No. Correction. Not 'Cast of honor'. Castor's Corner."

Angry sigh.

Regroup.

Let's try that again.

"Note: C-A-S-T-O-R-'-S. C-O-R-N-E-R. Cemetery. Ghost."

My phone beeped helpfully, then translated everything I just painfully spelled out into this rigamarole:

Cast of honor ghost in casserole. See money. Goat. Can I offer any further assistance?

Fuck. My. Literal. Life.

It was the lifelong bane of being born and raised in coastal New Jersey. The unshakable tendency to turn every "r" into an "aw" or just throw it out the window entirely.

I'd tried to retrain my phone's voice settings, but apparently it needed a Rosetta Stone for Jersey Witches to understand me.

Back to Miss Spritely.

She'd been principal of the Castor's Corner Elementary School for eighty years.

That was not an exaggeration. E-i-g-h-t-y.

She didn't look a day over sixty, which, considering she was technically pushing one hundred and ninety-seven, was impressive.

I blamed her profession for the early aging.

Spend nearly a century wrangling magical children through snack time and spontaneous spellcasting? Of course, you'd end up with grays, wrinkles, and a tendency to shriek like a harpy with a megaphone.

Honestly, I still flinched when she used her *disappointed in you* voice. The same one she'd used when I accidentally turned Tommy Wick into a toad in third grade.

Totally deserved, by the way. He told me my nose looked like a ski slope.

Still, even if she made my eardrums bleed and my blood pressure spike, Miss Spritely had a point.

It was my job to keep Castor's Corner safe. *Witch's oath and all.*

If something—*or someone*—was haunting the cemetery and scaring the kids, I had to investigate.

Tomorrow, I'd haul myself over there and see what the fuss was about. And if I did find a restless spirit throwing shade at first graders, I'd exorcise that gory ghoul right back into the afterlife before things escalated.

But right now?

I had no time to worry about cranky ghosts or vengeful field trip poltergeists.

I had a ritual to get to.

A bonfire to lead.

Wards to reinforce.

A protective barrier to rebuild.

And, Gaia, help me, I was already ten minutes late.

So, I did what any responsible mayor-Witch would do in my situation.

I gathered my skirt, muttered a quick ward to keep my shoes mud-free, and I ran like the hounds of hell were nipping at my heels.

Happened once.

And I do not recommend getting caught by those gnarly toothed bastards.

CHAPTER FOUR-EVIE

LET **Me Explain**

Every month, like clockwork—or, more accurately, like magically attuned Witches who couldn't afford to mess up the full moon schedule—the Trifecta gathered in the pine barrens behind town for our sacred ritual.

Yes, we lit a bonfire deep in the woods.

Yes, we danced under the full moon like fairytale rejects.

Yes, we chanted spells, sang our magic into the air, and—*because fate has a twisted sense of humor*—yes, we did it all butt-naked.

Birthday suits and boundary spells.

You know, totally normal Thursday night for a

thirty-something single mayor in a town full of paranormal misfits.

These rituals were sacred, old, and necessary.

They helped strengthen the wards around Castor's Corner, cloaking it from outsiders and keeping our supernatural community safe from meddling normals and wandering riff-raff.

In exchange, we offered Gaia—*the goddess supreme*—our bare buns and best intentions.

Which was great—*magically speaking*—except for the part where I forgot my ride was dead.

"Shit," I growled, coming to a full stop outside City Hall, staring at the empty space where my beloved but perpetually useless truck used to be.

I had no broomstick (blame budget cuts), no magical portal key, and no choice.

So, I ran.

That's right.

Ran.

Me.

Evelyn Castor.

Mayor of this fine town.

Forced to haul my fluff-and-caffeine-fueled ass eight city blocks to our sacred patch of pine scrub like a sweaty woodland creature in wedge sandals.

By the time I stumbled into the clearing, lungs wheezing, thighs protesting, and soul questioning every life choice I've ever made, I was running on fumes and sheer Witchy spite.

Note to self: never again eat a donut, a double bacon cheeseburger, chili cheese fries and a pumpkin muffin with cream cheese frosting on the same day as a full moon sprint.

That was just irresponsible adulting.

Salad tomorrow.

Ugh. Fine.

Salad and one cookie.

Maybe two.

"OMG, Evie!" Donatella shrieked, her voice echoing across the clearing like an angry banshee in yoga pants.

"You are so late," Maribella huffed, doing that annoying disappointed head shake while—*I kid you not*—shoving what was very clearly one of her sinfully good peanut butter chip cookies into her face like she thought I couldn't see her.

Heifer.

And not the magical sacred cow kind.

The straight-up snack-hoarding, sister-betraying kind.

I didn't have the breath to argue, so I just threw

them both a wide-eyed are-you-kidding-me look and motioned for them to get on with it while I tried not to collapse dramatically in a pile of forest mulch.

Donny, clearly still miffed, clucked at me like an angry hen for a few more seconds before flipping her long, dark hair over her shoulder and thankfully launching into the first spell to amplify the bonfire.

She shrugged off her short silk robe mid-incantation, because of course she did.

Like the fire wouldn't light properly unless her naked ass was perfectly framed under the moonlight.

Meanwhile, Maribella kicked off her chef's coat and pants in a well-practiced synchronicity of moves, revealing a pastel floral bra-and-panty set that somehow managed to be cute, flirty, and supportive.

I wasn't staring. I wasn't.

But the girl hit me with her pants and then blew me a raspberry when I looked up, so now I had to add *get revenge* and *ask where she got that lingerie* to my to-do list.

Later. Much later.

Like after I could breathe normally again and remember how to form complete sentences.

By this point, the fire had started to crackle,

golden-orange light spilling over the clearing like a spotlight summoned for moonlit mischief.

Our magic always sang louder during these gatherings.

There was something about shedding everything —*clothes, burdens, expectations*—and standing in your truest form under the stars.

It was powerful. Beautiful. Slightly drafty.

I started to shimmy out of my own clothes, grumbling the whole time about running and ghosts and the betrayal of peanut butter treats.

And just as I stepped closer to the flames, ready to join the others and officially begin the ritual, something shifted.

Not in the clearing.

Not in the bonfire.

In the air.

A ripple. A pull. A flutter at the base of my spine that felt nothing like cold wind and everything like a warning.

My magic prickled.

My heartbeat kicked up.

And that little voice in the back of my head—*the one that sounded suspiciously like Nonna*—whispered to me in my mind's eye.

Something's coming.

I didn't know what. Not yet.

But I had the sudden, undeniable feeling that this was going to be the last *normal* bonfire we had for a while.

And if the way the moon flickered overhead was any indication, then *normal* was about to get roasted.

CHAPTER FIVE-EVIE

IN THE PINE **Barrens**

With a few whispered words and a flick of her manicured fingers, Donny lit the fire. It crackled to life in the clearing like it was personally excited to see us.

I peeled off the rest of my clothes faster than a stripper on a time crunch—*dignity long gone and modesty overridden by magical protocol.*

Look, it's hard to feel embarrassed about nudity when you've done it every month for the last decade with the same two women who've seen you cry, rage, bloat, and curse your bra into flames at least once.

I glanced at Bella—*who gave me a knowing grin and*

a bounce of her blonde curls—and then at Donny, who nodded sharply like a general preparing to go to war.

Naked war.

This was it.

Our ritual.

Our purpose.

We were the Castor's Corner Witch Trifecta.

Three best friends.

Three magical misfits.

Three Witches bound to protect our supernatural small-town haven from anything and everything that might try to slip in uninvited.

Ghosts, Goblins, telemarketers—you name it.

Sure, we all had different strengths.

Donatella was the badass beauty guru with razor-sharp spells and a matching attitude.

Maribella was the culinary conjurer with frosting in her veins and a killer right hook.

And I was, well, me—but when we came together?

We were magic. *Literally.*

We danced, we chanted, we sang our power into the night air, letting it rise like incense into the stars.

I always felt self-conscious about this part—dancing was not my love language.

I was more *accidental hip check* than graceful enchantress.

But tonight, I found my rhythm.

The magic hummed through me like a melody I'd always known but only remembered during these moments.

My body moved in sync with the others, our magic overlapping and intertwining like chords in a song.

Mine was a cool, steady aqua with hints of shimmering lavender.

Bella's came out in bright pink streaks edged in glowing white.

Donny's magic sparkled gold, like a glitter bomb had gone off in a bottle of champagne.

Together, we painted the sky with color.

The bonfire rose higher, fed by our spellcasting.

Our lights swirled around us, flowing from our fingertips into the flames, rising to form a protective dome over our town.

A beacon to Gaia.

A warning to outsiders.

We were doing it.

Strengthening the wards.

Keeping Castor's Corner hidden.

Keeping everyone safe.

I was in it. Fully present. Fully powered. Buzzing with purpose and pride.

I loved this part. The trance-like state where it felt like even the trees were humming approval, the fireflies pulsing in sync with our chants, the whole forest breathing with us. Magic whispered across my skin like warm mist.

I tilted my head back, eyes closed, and belted out the chant:

"Gaia, grant us
Space to be,
Keep the outsiders out,
We offer thee
Our hearts and devotion,
To truly be
The corner where casting
Is done freely."

Okay, fine.

The rhyme was a little *fourth-grade poetry contest,* but whatever.

It worked.

And hey, at least I didn't drop an f-bomb mid-spell this time.

Nonna would've zapped my left cheek if I rhymed shit with lit again. And not in the fun way.

Anyway.

The magic swelled. The colors spun. I was riding the high, wrapped in moonlight and the power of sisterhood and sparkles when—*something shifted.*

Not just in the air.

Not just in the earth.

In the spell.

There was a *ripple.*

Something foreign.

Earthy. Electric.

Not ours.

I felt it—it was an energy that didn't belong to the Trifecta.

It wasn't malevolent.

It was *vibrant.*

Wild. Intrusive.

Alive in the way only the deeply confident or incredibly clueless could be.

And there wasn't just one source.

There were *three.*

Simultaneously, Maribella, Donny, and I stopped mid-gyration.

The fire still roared behind us, casting glittery shadows across our bare skin.

We locked eyes.

The energy pulsed again.

And then—*together, as if choreographed*—we turned.

Standing just outside the glow of our bonfire, watching us like they'd stumbled onto a live-action fantasy calendar, were three of the hottest men I had ever seen.

And I don't mean hot *like attractive in a rugged, lumberjack-adjacent way.*

I mean HOT.

Capital H, capital O, capital T.

But more like HOLY-HELL-WHAT-EVEN-ARE-THEY HOT.

They looked like they'd been carved out of midnight and muscle.

All broad shoulders, wicked jawlines, and simmering supernatural energy.

One had thick tousled hair and storm-gray eyes that locked onto me like a predator spotting its favorite snack.

Another leaned against a tree like it owed him rent, exuding cocky confidence and low-key danger.

The third, well, he had the kind of slow, smoldering gaze that made my inner thighs consider filing a formal complaint.

"Holy—" I started, the word dying in my throat.

"Gaia," Maribella breathed, eyes wide as saucers.

"Have mercy," Donatella muttered, sounding almost reverent.

There we were—*completely naked, mid-ritual, magic practically dripping off us like glitter and pheromones*—and these three supernatural smoke shows were staring at us like starving men at a fried chicken buffet.

And just like that? Realization dawned.

We weren't alone.

The spell had been *breached*.

The wards *cracked*.

And if I wasn't mistaken, fate had just RSVP'd to our moonlit naked dance party.

Shit was about to get very complicated.

But before I got into that, I needed to understand what I was looking at.

Man #1 stepped forward—tall, broad, and built like a professional rugby player who moonlighted as a Greek god.

The kind of man who could carry three kegs, fix your roof, and ruin your life with a smile. I bit back a groan.

I had a thing for muscular men. Who didn't?

But this one? He was a walking, talking, six-foot-something-tall mistake in the making.

He had tousled dark brown hair, sun-kissed skin, and eyes that glowed.

Silver. Freaking. Eyes.

And they were locked on me like I was the last slice of birthday cake at a coven sleepover.

His grin? Wolfish. Dangerous.

The kind that said, *I will ruin your panties and then your peace of mind.*

Good Gaia.

I was naked.

In the woods.

And clearly not getting enough action.

My libido perked up like it had just been called off the bench.

No. Down, girl. Not the time.

Maybe I'd try Windr after all, even if magical dating apps gave me hives.

Who was I kidding? I couldn't do casual to save my life.

I fell hard, got weird, and usually ended up hexing their toothbrushes after they ghosted me.

So, I stuffed my carnal instincts into a mental broom closet and turned my attention to his companions.

Bachelor #2? He was the biggest of the three, with dark hair dusted with gray and a neatly trimmed beard.

His warm brown eyes were calm, kind, and *dammit, Daddy.*

He radiated protective energy and smelled faintly of cinnamon and competence.

And Bachelor #3 had messy blond hair like he'd just run his fingers through it for fun, and green eyes that sparkled in the moonlight—*like a forest sprite who bench-pressed trees for fun.*

He looked adorably bewildered by our state of undress.

Then the first one—*the silver-eyed panty-melter*—opened his mouth.

"Excuse me, the name's Jaxson," he said, dripping with Southern charm and a sinfully sexy smolder, "and I was wonderin' if you could help us? Is this Maccon City?"

Oh no.

Oh no no.

The other two at least had the decency to avert their gazes, but not this guy.

He kept his laser-focused eyes on me, drinking me in like I was a triple shot of espresso on a Monday morning.

My entire body lit up like it had just been plugged into a magical power grid.

And I hated it.

Kinda.

"No. This is not Maccon City. You're in Castor's

Corner. I'm Evelyn Castor—mayor and pissed-off citizen—and unless one of you brought a fire extinguisher, a peace offering, or a damn portal key to reverse a magical disaster, I suggest you stop smiling and start explaining," I snapped, annoyed at him, at fate, and mostly at my own body for being so damn interested.

I let my hands settle on my hips, resisting the urge to grab a robe—*or a pitchfork.*

"Well? Care to tell me what the fuck you're doing on protected land?"

Sure, I was furious about the invasion—but honestly?

I was more pissed at him for knocking me off-balance with that stupid smolder and sinful drawl.

That man should come with a warning label.

Or at least some sort of magical bell so a girl could mentally prepare.

I stepped in front of my girls—*because apparently, I was the naked human shield now*—and lifted my chin.

Defiant. Fierce. Utterly exposed, but still the boss.

Not that he was even looking at them.

His silver gaze was all for me.

His friends, however, were not-so-subtly eyeing

Bella and Donny like fated mate energy was just wafting on the breeze.

Ugh. Whatever.

It wasn't like I was flattered by his covetous gaze or anything. I wasn't about to blush like some flustered fairytale virgin.

I had nothing to be ashamed of.

This was my magic, my moment, my body.

He could look all he wanted, but I wasn't backing down.

I squared my shoulders and scowled. "Well? What are you looking at?"

He smiled slow. Too slow.

Like he knew he was dangerous and liked it that way.

"Perfection, Darlin'. Pure perfection," he said, voice so rich and slow it might as well have been poured over hotcakes.

I shivered.

Gaia help me, the man had a Southern accent as thick as molasses and ten times as sticky.

I was weak.

Physically weak.

I clenched my jaw to keep from swooning right into the bonfire.

"But what the Goddess are you doing here? This

is sacred land," I snapped, a little more breathlessly than I wanted.

"It sure is," he agreed.

Of course, he's obnoxiously cute, too.

"Didn't anyone ever tell you it's rude to stare?" I added.

He gave a slow blink and shrugged like a rogue cowboy with no shame.

"Honey, if I stopped starin' at you, they'd revoke my man card. Now, what are you girls doin' out here, dancin' in the moonlight?"

I snorted.

"First off, we're not 'girls.' We're fully grown Witches. Second, these are our woods. You're trespassing."

The green-eyed blond one finally spoke. "Uh, excuse us. We're sorry, ladies. We didn't mean to intrude."

At least he had manners.

"We were just trying to get to Maccon City. Took a wrong turn somewhere, then our truck got a flat. Engine just went poof," he said, scratching his neck.

"Actually, it was the weirdest thing. We hit a hydrant sitting about six-inches out from the sidewalk. Anyway, we saw the fire. Thought maybe someone needed help," he stammered.

Damn it, Dick, you and those stupid fire hydrants.

I mentally cursed-out my ex.

"Um, did you say you three were Witches?" he added after a beat.

"Oh my Gaia," Bella squeaked. "Shit on a shingle. They're Shifters, Evie!"

"Course we are," Mr. Sexy drawled, grinning with all his teeth.

Too many teeth. Very Wolfy of him.

"Didn't you have a spare tire?" I asked, more annoyed than I had any right to be.

"The spare was flat too," he said, still ogling me like I was his birthday wish.

"We were more worried about the fire spreadin'."

"Hey, are you guys firefighters?" Donatella asked hopefully.

"Have been," the older, gigantic one offered, his deep voice surprisingly gentle. "Among other things. We've all worn a lot of hats. Cops. EMTs. Handymen. I was even a baker for a while."

"Jacks of all trades," Maribella whispered, eyes wide with curiosity and a little too much excitement.

Mr. Smolder stepped forward, sweeping into an infuriatingly charming bow that should not have worked but absolutely did.

"Name's Jaxson. Jaxson Reid, at your service."

"You said that already," I grumbled, but he just winked.

Smug bastard.

He gestured to the big, soft-spoken one. "That's Ryan McLeod."

And to the blond. "And this is Conrad Boman."

Great. Now all three panty-melters had names.

And voices.

Mr. Silver Eyes had dimples, too.

I was a sucker for dimples.

His peeked out when he grinned.

And if I wasn't careful, I might find myself attracted to him.

I could not afford to let that happen.

Too late. Shit.

"So, you ladies really are Witches, then?" Ryan McLeod asked, his gravelly voice doing things to my spine that should've required a permit.

He was the big one.

Broad shoulders, deep brown eyes, streaks of silver in his hair and beard that somehow made him look more dangerous and more comforting all at once.

Like a sexy lumberjack-turned-guardian-angel who'd chop your firewood and tuck you in at night. *With cookies.*

"You got a problem with that?" Donatella snapped, sparks flicking off her fingertips like she was a human sparkler with a grudge.

Poor guy visibly flinched.

"Nope, I just, uh…" He coughed. "Never met any with your, um, *assets.*"

That did it. I snorted. Actually snorted.

And then laughed, because Donny's glare was somewhere between *I will smite you* and *I might kiss you after I fry your eyebrows off.*

It was adorable, in a someone's-gonna-get-scorched kind of way.

But Bella, ever the voice of sugar-laced reason, elbowed me in the ribs hard enough to knock the humor right out of me.

Right. Not the time to flirt.

Or snort-laugh.

Or imagine what a man like Ryan could do with those huge hands. Focus, Evie.

I snapped my fingers in the air.

"Easy," I said quietly, glancing between my besties.

Donny still looked ready to unleash some serious lightning bitch energy, but Ryan lifted both palms like a man familiar with high-voltage women.

"No, ma'am," he said quickly. "No problem at all."

His voice was so deep it practically echoed in my pelvis.

And judging by the way his eyes were glued to Donny, he definitely didn't mind her attitude.

Or her curves.

Or her brazen magic.

Hell, he looked like he wanted to write her a sonnet about it.

Donny pointed a glowing finger at him anyway, but I slapped her hand down before she turned Mr. Shifter into a toasted marshmallow.

Ryan chuckled once—*short, surprised*—and I blinked.

His eyes. Were they glowing?

No—wait—yes.

A flash of gold shimmered in those deep browns, like embers catching in the dark. Oof.

"Donny! Control yourself," Maribella scolded, clearly amused but trying to play the responsible Witch.

I cleared my throat and stepped forward, putting a little more mayoral steel in my voice.

"If you boys would kindly give us a little privacy," I said coolly, "we'll see about getting you back on the road to Maccon City."

It was the right thing to say.

Logical. Professional.

So why did it sting a little?

Odd.

Ryan and Conrad turned instantly, like gentlemen who knew when to bow out—but of course, Jaxson Reid didn't budge.

That grin of his stretched wider, and I swear to Gaia, the man slow-blinked at me.

Like a smug, sexy predator basking in the moonlight.

Then he let his eyes—*those ridiculous, molten silver eyes*—roam.

From my face to my toes and back up again, nice and slow, like he was mentally tattooing my body for reference.

It was obscene. It was infuriating.

It was *really, really effective.*

My nipples hardened like traitors.

My stomach did somersaults.

Butterflies? No. These were fighter jets doing loop-the-loops behind my belly button. From one look.

One. Fucking. Look.

Shit. This was not good.

It wasn't just that he was hot—though, yes, he was hotter than Satan's sauna.

It was the way he looked at me.

Like he already knew what I looked like in every position, in every shade of moonlight, and had plans.

It had been a long time since someone looked at me like that.

Scratch that.

I don't think anyone had ever looked at me like that.

And yes, I had a rechargeable boyfriend named Ernest and a healthy appreciation for privacy.

But this was *different*.

Dangerous.

Like my defenses were being dismantled by dimples and Southern charm.

Nope. Nope nope nope.

Never again.

I'd made that mistake with Dick Daniels—may his beard oil curdle in Hell.

Just because a man looked good and knew how to charm didn't mean he was worth a damn.

Dick had played the long game—*flattery, flowers, flirty spells*—and then bailed the second I got too real.

I'd sworn off dating, relationships, and anything with a penis and a pulse.

I had my friends, my magic, and Ernest, thank you very much.

But apparently, my hoo-ha had not gotten the memo.

Because she was currently composing a welcome speech for Jaxson Reid and trying to manifest a hotel room with a jacuzzi tub and zero witnesses.

Focus, Evie.

Note to self: Use his actual name.

Do not call him *Hottie McDoMeRightNow* in your head.

Because, honestly? That was not helping.

Not even a little.

As if he knew I was silently reprimanding myself, the bastard chuckled.

And good Gaia, that sound.

Deep and masculine and delicious. It vibrated. Through me. *Into me.*

Suddenly, I was picturing things.

Things involving six-and-a-half feet of bare Shifter, a bowl of chocolate pudding, and a very, very small spoon.

I swallowed. Hard.

Yup, I was in trouble.

Big, broad-shouldered, pudding-coated trouble.

And I had no one to blame but myself.

CHAPTER SIX-EVIE

STILL BUTT ASS **Naked in the Pine Barrens**

My face was on fire by the time I was fully dressed again—which, to be clear, was about twenty seconds too late to salvage my dignity.

Not that there was much left of it after being caught buck naked mid-moon chant by three unreasonably attractive strangers.

I turned just in time to see Donny and Maribella already re-robed and whispering like two middle schoolers with a dirty secret.

Bella was doing that wide-eyed thing she did when she was scandalized but intrigued, while Donny's smirk could have curdled fresh milk.

They were dousing the bonfire with synchronized flicks of their fingers and the kind of Witchy urgency that said *we're in trouble, but also, there're hot guys here.*

Maribella motioned me over, her voice a sharp hiss. "How did they get here, Evie?"

I blinked. "You mean, tonight or like *existentially?* Because I feel like I might need therapy to answer that second one."

"Focus!" she snapped.

"I don't know!" I said, throwing my hands up. "Maybe they have really good GPS?"

"Do you think maybe we let our guard down?" Donny added. "You know, when we were waiting for you?"

Oof.

Right in the guilt center.

I felt it, hot and heavy, sitting in my chest like the chili cheese fries I absolutely should not have eaten earlier.

If this was my fault—*and it was totally feeling like it might be*—I had to own it.

Responsibility was my middle name.

Well, it was actually Marie, but whatever.

Same vibe.

"Maybe," I muttered. "Probably. Okay, yes. I suck. Let's all write it in the sky and move on."

Donny just gave me a look. You know the one.

Equal parts I told you so and I will hex your favorite flats.

"They are kinda hot, though," Maribella said dreamily, biting her lip and staring at the blond one like he was her latest no-calorie brownie experiment.

And look, one day she's gonna get it right and create a guilt-free chocolate chip cookie that tastes like magic and not sad cardboard—but today was not that day.

Until then, my thighs and I were locked in a battle of wills that I was definitely losing.

Ugh.

One whiff of a cinnamon roll and my ass doubled in volume like it had a yeast starter of its own.

Aunt Edna's genes were strong.

That woman could take out a buffet table and a folding chair with one good spin in a crowded room.

"Alright," I said, squaring my shoulders. "Let's get some answers."

I turned to face the trespassers—*aka, the human-shaped sin parade*—and tried to remember I was the mayor.

Not a hormonal mess in yoga pants.

Which, by the way, were clinging in all the wrong places post-bonfire.

"So, your truck crapped out on you?" I asked, approaching with the cautious authority of a woman who'd once dated a Wizard and barely survived the emotional trauma.

Back in my clothes, I felt a small ounce of control return.

At least now I could focus on their eyes without wondering if my boobs were bouncing in time with my heartbeat.

Priorities.

The oldest one—*Ryan, who looked like a teddy bear who moonlighted as a lumberjack*—gave me a sheepish look and rubbed the back of his neck.

"Actually, ma'am," he said, voice thick with Southern shame, "I think it kinda did, but only after we hit that oddly spaced hydrant. It happened so fast. Right when we made that wrong turn into your little town. That's when the tire blew. Then the engine just died."

I narrowed my eyes.

"You sure that's what you hit?"

Like I had any doubt.

He looked at the others for support. Didn't get any. They all looked like kids caught sneaking cookies before dinner.

"Yep. A fire hydrant," he finally muttered. "It was just, uh, kind of in the road?"

"Dammit, Evie," Donny barked, marching up beside me like she was ready to write a ticket with fire.

"Well," Jaxson added, sounding genuinely baffled. "It was six inches off the curb. Weirdest placement I've ever seen. Who does that?"

Shit.

Oh no.

I felt my face twitch.

My left eye might've actually spasmed.

Fuck.

Stanley was never going to stop giving me shit about this. Especially after I told him I had it handled.

Sigh. Damned fire hydrant debacle.

"So, you mean to tell us," Donny started, "that this all happened because of that creep, Dick Daniels, and his brilliant idea to relocate the hydrants for *optimal magical access*, or some bullshit," she said, using air quotes.

"Donny, he told me it was standard in elite supernatural jurisdictions. And I'd believed him. Sue me!" I replied.

But I still felt dumb about it. At the time, I was high on infatuation and low on critical thinking.

Damn that special ops Wizard and his dumb, sexy beard.

"Stupid freaking lying-ass Wizard," I muttered under my breath.

"Excuse me?" Jaxson asked, grinning.

"Nothing," I barked, too loudly. "Don't worry about it. I'm just *allergic to bullshit*. It flares up sometimes."

Donny snorted.

Bella coughed to hide her laugh.

And the Shifters all exchanged a look.

The kind that said, we have definitely walked into a magical mess of epic proportions.

Which, to be fair, *they had.*

And I had a sinking feeling that our troubles were just getting started.

"Ma'am?" Conrad, the blond one, asked, scratching his blond locks.

"Okay. It's nothing. Just a stupid mistake I made, and I've been working to correct it for the last six months," I said, shaking my eyes at the memory of that failed relationship.

"Made, as in the past?" Jaxson asked, a little too interested for someone who just met me.

"OMG! I swear if I ever see Dick again, I will castrate the fucker!" Donny growled.

All three Shifters covered their man parts, scowling at her vehement promise.

I couldn't help my laugh. Neither could Maribella.

"No worries, boys, she doesn't mean your family jewels," Bella said, smirking.

"Maribella is right," I inserted. "You see, our last fire chief was a Wizard, and he thought moving the hydrants off the curb was an efficient way of getting the firetrucks closer to one in case of emergency. He didn't bother thinking what that meant to other motorists and used our non-relationship to get his ideas pushed through City Council."

"Non-relationship?" Jaxson inquired, but I ignored his nosy ass.

I was not about to wax poetic on my failed dating history.

"Anyway," I said, taking control of the narrative. "You have my apologies, and the city will pay for the repairs to your tire and rim if there was any damage," I added begrudgingly.

"Why should the city pay?" Jaxson asked, crossing his arms and causing his impressive biceps and triceps to flex beneath the cotton of his shirt.

Yowza.

"Well, it's our fault," I explained. "Dick moved those hydrants using the city without going through proper channels. I have been moving them back one by one with my magic, but some buggers are harder than others."

"Ain't that the truth," Maribella whispered, and again I giggled.

"Damn it," I growled, slapping my BFF's hand. "Get a grip," I whispered.

"What did you ladies say the name of this town was again?" Jaxson put the question to us all, but I felt his stare settle on me.

Again, my girly bits went haywire, but I played it off.

Cool as a cucumber.

Of course, my eyes went right to his, uh, *cucumber*, and I was shocked at the enormous bulge I spied beneath his tight-fitting blue jeans.

I cleared my throat and forced myself to look at his face, ignoring the pleasant scents of lemon and basil that wafted my way.

"I already told you, it's *Castor's Corner*. I'm Evie Castor, mayor."

"Well, Madam Mayor," Jaxson replied, hand extended as he invaded my space.

I hated having to look up at tall people, but being five foot three, if I was pushing it, that meant I usually had to.

The lemon basil fragrance grew stronger, and I recognized it as coming from him.

Holy cow.

"Wolf, actually," he replied, and I swallowed hard.

The sexy sonovabitch had read my mind.

Shit.

This was so not good.

"So, Madam Mayor," he continued. "What do we need to do if we wanna stay for a while?"

Me.

The thought was on the tip of my tongue, but I managed to keep my lips shut.

Didn't matter. He heard me anyway.

"That is something I look forward to taking care of, Darlin'," the Wolf drawled.

Fuck. Me.

Yes, please.

Shit.

I closed my eyes as a pang of lust washed over me.

It was the *Darlin'* that did it.

I felt him move into my space and closed my eyes even tighter, hoping to ward him away.

"Anything you need, Madam Mayor, I got it right here."

And there went my panties.

CHAPTER SEVEN-JAXSON

WASN'T LIKE we planned to roll into Castor's Corner, New Jersey.

Hell, it wasn't even on the damn map.

Me, Ryan, and Conrad had packed up our shit and set our GPS for Maccon City—*the unofficial supernatural capital of the Northeast.*

Big Pack territory.

Plenty of opportunities.

Shifters welcome.

That was the goal.

But fate? She had other plans.

One minute we're cruisin' along, shooting the breeze and arguing over gas station jerky brands.

Next thing I know, I see it.

A goddamn fire made of pink, teal, and gold

sparking into the night sky like a glitter bomb set off by a horny unicorn.

I slammed the brakes.

The truck hydroplaned—*with no water present.*

Ryan cursed.

Conrad hissed.

Then bam—front right tire hits a hydrant.

An oddly placed one, I might add.

Truck dies right there.

Dead as a doornail.

That's when I knew something magical was pulling us in.

So we followed the scent.

Wolf senses locked in. Magic and something sweeter—*like honey, citrus, and summer sweat.*

And then we saw them.

Three Witches.

Naked. Glorious. Powerful.

But I didn't see three.

I saw one.

Curves for days, attitude for miles, and a mouth I wanted to taste in every filthy way I could dream up.

Brown hair whipping in the moonlight.

Magic sparkling off her skin.

Snarky as hell.

Evie Castor.

Mayor.

Witch.

My fated mate.

And yeah, she doesn't know it yet.

Hell, she barely looked me in the eye without a scowl. But I felt the pull deep in my bones.

The second I saw her? My Wolf snarled.

Mine.

She can fight it.

Be all prickly and political.

Doesn't change a damn thing.

Because I'm already gone for her.

I wanna lick her from head to toe.

Want her in my lap, my bed, my life.

Wanna hear her moan my name while I sink my teeth into her soft skin and give her my claiming mark.

Stamp her with my scent so no other male even thinks about lookin' her way.

And when she finally lets me in?

Game over.

'Cause I'm Jaxson Reid.

I don't run from fate.

I hunt it down, wrap it up in my arms, and never let it go.

And Evie?

She's already mine.

I watched her walk away—Evie.

All curves and confidence, muttering under her breath like she was cursing me in three languages.

Goddess, I hoped she was.

I'd take her hex over any blessing just to keep her eyes on me.

I let out a low growl under my breath and turned back to the guys.

Ryan was still staring at the one with lightning in her fingertips—Donatella, I think Evie called her.

And Conrad? The big guy was practically vibrating, eyes glued to the bubbly blonde with cookie crumbs on her cheek. Maribella.

Goddess help him, I think he already imprinted on her over baked goods.

I pulled them both aside, behind a scraggly pine and out of Witch earshot.

Didn't want to be singed before I made my case.

"Alright," I said low, voice serious now. "I'm stayin'."

Ryan blinked. "Stayin' the night?"

I gave him a look. "Nah, Ry. I mean I'm staying. In this town. For good. She's here."

"The mayor?" Conrad asked, brow furrowing. "Evie?"

I nodded once. "She's it. My mate. I felt it the second I saw her—hell, maybe even before. Like my soul slammed the brakes before the truck did."

Ryan let out a soft breath.

"Shit."

Conrad grinned.

"Called it. Knew something was up the second you got all weird and smiley."

I shoved his shoulder. "Shut up. So, what about you two? You in?"

They didn't even hesitate.

Ryan glanced toward Donny—who was still glaring daggers at him while aggressively stuffing her robe into a tote bag—and gave a slow, crooked smile.

"Yeah. I'm in. I don't care if she fries me where I stand. That woman's a goddess in a silk robe laced with sass."

Conrad nodded toward Maribella, who was sneakily eating another cookie and acting like no one noticed.

"She's sunshine and snacks. I'll follow her into a volcano."

I snorted.

"Y'all are whipped already, and we haven't even had breakfast."

Ryan shrugged.

"Speak for yourself. I'll be cookin' her pancakes by sunrise if she lets me."

We grinned at each other, three grown-ass Shifters caught in fate's fishing net like love-struck fools.

But we weren't running.

We were staying.

In Castor's Corner.

With our Witches.

Now we just had to convince them.

And pray to Gaia they didn't turn us into toads before we got the chance.

CHAPTER EIGHT-EVIE

THE DAY **After Everything Changed**

I leaned in closer to the mirror, one hand braced on the sink while the other gingerly peeled back my eyelid.

"Oh, holy shitballs," I groaned.

It was worse than I thought. I looked like I'd gone ten rounds with a peppermint stick-wielding raccoon and lost.

My left eye was an angry, puffy red, and my lashes were clumped together like they'd been dipped in mucus and shame.

"I told you it was bad," Donny said, still dramatically gasping like she wasn't the one who once set her own eyebrows on fire trying to enchant a curling iron.

"You should glam it," Maribella suggested helpfully, coming up behind me and placing a soothing hand on my shoulder.

"Just a little glamour. No one has to know your optic nerve had a spa day with Listerine."

"Can't," I moaned, pushing a clump of soggy hair behind my ear. "Glamours don't work right when the sight's acting up. I'll end up looking like a pirate with a lazy eye. Or worse, I'll look like I went three rounds with *Dick Daniels*."

Both women gasped.

"You take that back," Donny snapped, clutching her chest like I'd personally insulted her houseplants.

"You're right," I said, rinsing my face again and patting it dry with the nearest towel. "That was uncalled for. I apologize to your houseplants. And to pirates."

Donatella grumbled under her breath, then flopped dramatically onto my couch like a fainting Victorian duchess.

"We need to talk about the Shifters, Evie."

"Oh, don't you think I know that?" I groaned. "I spent the whole night dreaming about that smug, muscled menace licking brownie batter off my—"

"Too much info!" Maribella sang, slapping her

hands over her ears. "Seriously, I will never look at brownies the same way again."

Donny sat up. "You're not denying it, though."

"Denying what?"

"That you felt the pull."

I bit my lip.

"Of course I felt the pull. You could power the whole damn Eastern Seaboard with that level of chemistry. But that doesn't mean I'm ready to hop aboard the mating train and ride it to O-Town."

"Well, maybe it's not about you being ready," Maribella said gently, her eyes suspiciously soft. "Maybe it's about fate being ready."

"Oh, gag me with a spork," I muttered, crossing my arms. "Don't get all poetic on me. You know I can't handle that before coffee."

"Speaking of," Donny stood and headed for the kitchen. "I'm making a pot. You look like death and sound like denial."

"Thank you, always such a ray of fucking sunshine."

While she clattered around with my kettle like she owned the place—*which, to be fair, she kind of did half the time*—I sank into the nearest armchair and pulled a throw pillow onto my lap like it could shield me from the clusterfuck of my life.

I had way too much shit to deal with as it was. My to-do list for the day was making me twitch.

I had:

1. One angry principal and a horde of panicked parents blowing up my inbox.

2. A town paper claiming I was leading full moon orgies in the forest.

3. Three sexy-as-sin Shifters stranded on my turf.

4. A very strong suspicion I'd been singled out by one of them without so much as a how-do-you-do.

5. A literal pink eye from hell.

And it was only 7:17 AM.

I needed a plan.

A solid, responsible, definitely-not-panty-melting plan.

Something mayoral. Something mature.

"So what's the move?" Donny asked, dropping a mug of hot coffee into my hands like a lifeline.

I took a sip. "First, I fix my eye."

"Then?"

"Then I handle the cemetery situation and tell the Shifters to keep their ridiculously hot, magical, possibly mate-claiming selves far, far away from the Trifecta."

Maribella raised a skeptical brow.

"You gonna say all that to *his* face?"

I paused, thinking about silver eyes, molasses drawls, and the way his biceps flexed when he crossed his arms.

"No," I admitted. "I'm gonna send an email."

Donny snorted so hard she nearly spit her coffee.

"Coward," she said fondly.

"Realist," I countered. "Besides, I've got a town to run. And there's no way some sinfully handsome Wolf Shifter is gonna derail that."

At that exact moment, my phone pinged with a text. I glanced at the screen.

JAXSON "HOTTIE" REID

> Morning, Darlin'. You dream about me? I sure as hell dreamed about you. How about you come on over for a little breakfast?

My stomach flipped.

My eye twitched.

And somewhere, deep down in my soul, my magic whispered.

Evelyn Castor, you're so screwed.

I turned my cell phone upside down and pushed all thoughts of his furry hotness out of my head.

Then, I closed my eyes and focused on a healing spell.

Or, well, I tried.

"Evie! No!"

I stopped mid-chant and grabbed the compact Bella was holding to look at myself.

"Holy Befana! Oh, my Gaia!" I spat, staring at my reflection in abject horror.

I'd invoked both the ancestral Witches of my foremothers, La Befana, and Gaia herself.

The myth of my family's *Old World Village Witch* was still talked about even in mortal circles as the Witch who gifted good children with presents during the holidays.

Of course, the Befana I knew was hundreds of years old and gorgeous as ever, think an eternal Sophia Loren.

These days, she lived in a multimillion-dollar brownstone in Little Italy and was in charge of all magical beings in the Northeast under the Morrigan herself.

Among her several holdings was one of the world's largest Italian pastry franchises.

Mama B's Pasticceria.

Her cannolis were fucking fabulous.

Still, she wouldn't catch wind of the profanity spoken in her name.

Gaia, however, was another story.

But who could blame me for cursing, possibly

pissing off the great benevolent Gaia herself?

I looked like a traffic accident.

Did I mention she was perfect in all ways?

I peeked up at the ceiling and window and noted no storm clouds.

Hopefully, she missed my little faux pas and had no plans to zap my ass.

Mouthwash in the eye was enough of a physical trial for one morning.

"Dammit, Donny, I'm late as it is, just fix it already," I grumbled.

"Fifteen minutes," Donny announced like she was a Fairy Godmother on a deadline. "That's all you get. I have a hair appointment with Emily at noon and a vendetta against my nosy neighbor, Mr. Adams, that won't plot itself."

I grumbled something unintelligible as she waved her hands over me, muttering a glamor incantation that sounded suspiciously like it included the words *for the love of all things holy, get it together, Evie.*

The pink eye disappeared in a shimmery flash of gold, and then—*because Donny was a perfectionist*—my hair sprang into fat, shiny waves that bounced like I'd just walked off a Pantene commercial.

"Don't say I never do anything for you," she said

smugly, tossing a brush into her purse like a mic drop.

"You're a goddess. A terrifying, foul-mouthed, miracle-working goddess."

"Damn straight."

I kissed her cheek and bolted, leaving her to terrorize my kitchen cabinets for something sweet.

That woman had a sixth sense for hidden cookies.

Outside, the summer air was warm and thick with the scent of honeysuckle, and birds chirped like they weren't living in a town full of magical chaos.

I tugged my sunglasses over my newly fixed eye and adjusted the strap on my oversized purse.

Then I started walking.

To the cemetery.

Because that was the totally normal, definitely-not-spooky destination of choice for any small-town mayor with a haunted inbox and a libido in full rebellion over a sexy Wolf Shifter.

Seriously, if someone had told twelve-year-old me that adulthood meant haunted clock towers, horny Wolves, and municipal scandals involving off-kilter hydrants, I'd have packed my bags and applied for Fairy Godmother school.

But no, here I was.

Mayor Evelyn Castor, trying to solve supernatural mysteries with a half-melted protein bar in my bag, zero backup, and the lingering memory of a Southern drawl that made my ovaries chant like Gregorian monks.

Miss Spritely's complaint had been pretty straightforward—kids were showing up late to school, dragging their feet, and looking pale.

But no one was sick.

No buses were late.

No magical curses detected.

Just kids stalling out near the cemetery. Which, by the way, had been quiet for decades.

Until now.

And the phrase *junkless wonder*? Still a mystery.

I picked up the pace and tried to shake off the creep factor.

This was Castor's Corner. Weird was the status quo.

I mean, we already had a slew of madness I could barely keep straight—*and I was mayor!*

For example, Castor's Corner was renowned for having:

A sentient apple tree that only produced fruit if you complimented it first.

A ghost who haunted the DMV and could only be appeased with glitter pens.

And a recurring magical event every decade where the entire town relived the same exact day for seven straight days. We just called it Déjà Voodoo Week.

Honestly, this town was exhausting.

But it was mine.

And if there was something going down in the cemetery—*another prank, a ghost, or, Gaia forbid, some cursed crypt creature trolling for juvie souls*—I'd deal with it.

I just hoped it didn't involve more naked rituals or encounters with panty-melting Shifters.

Because I was fresh out of clean underwear, and emotionally?

Let's just say I was one more sexily drawled *Darlin'* away from hurling myself into a salt circle and calling it a day.

With that incredibly comforting thought in mind, I reached the cemetery gates.

They creaked open all by themselves.

Of course they did.

"Castor's Corner," I muttered to myself, stepping through. "Where the weird never sleeps, and neither do I."

CHAPTER NINE-EVIE

OF COURSE, I should've known better than to think I'd make it through a single peaceful cemetery stroll without a run-in from my past.

Literally.

"Hello there, Evie."

Ugh. That voice.

That smug, nasal, nose-high voice I'd recognize anywhere.

I didn't even have to turn around to know Dick Daniels—*yes, that's really his name*—was side-stepping it up next to me like a smug little Goblin who just stepped out of a cologne ad for toxic masculinity.

Ex-boyfriend.

Former Fire Chief.

Current walking cautionary tale.

"What are you doing in there?" he asked, peering through the iron gates like a paparazzo outside Buckingham Palace.

I didn't dignify him with an answer right away.

Just gave him my patented I'd-rather-hug-a-porcupine glare and kept walking.

You'd think after ghosting me post-breakup—*and nearly burning down the north side of town with that stunt involving flammable warding oil*—he'd get the universal hint to go haunt someone else's emotional trauma.

Alas, Dick was nothing if not persistent.

And short-penised.

As was the case with most fire-slinging Warlocks I'd dated.

That was a joke. Mostly. Probably.

"I said, what are you doing in a cemetery, Evelyn?"

The way he said my full name grated on my nerves like silver on a chalkboard.

"Hello Richard," I said, plastering on a smile so fake it belonged on a reality TV show. "I'm working. You remember what that is, right? Doing your job instead of flirting your way through zoning permits?"

He blinked. Opened his mouth like he had something clever to say, but that was never the case now, was it?

"Good mornin', Madam Mayor."

And just like that, the universe hit me with a plot twist in the form of six-foot-plus of Wolf Shifter hotness, wrapped in a cotton shirt, tight jeans, and lemon-basil sex appeal.

I turned and promptly forgot how to breathe.

Oh. Oh, holy full moon and flaming broomsticks.

It was him alright.

Jaxson Reid.

Silver eyes.

A voice made of dark roast and temptation.

Shoulders like he could carry my emotional baggage and a small village.

I mean, I'm not usually the type to swoon—*I leave that to the gothic heroines in tragic novels*—but damn if my knees didn't do a little dip.

He was prettier than me.

And I use highlighter and glamour spells.

Dick—*the Wizard, not the euphemism (though also applicable)*—sniffled like a toddler with allergies, clearly sensing the incoming alpha energy radiating off my new problem.

"This fella botherin' you, Darlin'?"

Holy. Hotness.

"Who, Dick? No, um, Dick doesn't, um, bother me," I whispered, sounding like a breathless moron.

Ugh, Evie, stop it!

Jaxson nodded at me, then turned his silver stare on Dick.

And as if on cue, Dick backed up.

Jaxson moved forward.

Two more steps, closing the space between us.

And Dick actually jogged backwards.

Like someone shouted *free laser hair removal* in his general direction.

To be fair, Dick had a slight unibrow problem.

Okay, fine, it looked like a black prison bus parked across his forehead.

Snort.

"You sure you're alright, Darlin'?" Jaxson asked, all sincerity.

"Yup," I replied.

Watching my ex back up—literally taking five steps backwards, all because a Werewolf growled in my general direction?

Yeah. That kind of did it for me.

It was only seven in the morning and already my day was improving by leaps, bounds, and magically enhanced pheromones.

I glanced at the sky.

Then, I turned to the towering Shifter, my grin stretched so wide I probably looked half-feral, half-dazed.

And that, of course, was exactly the moment my stomach decided to flip like a damn pancake on Beltane brunch duty.

And not just from the sizzling heat of Jaxson Reid's Southern drawl.

No, it was the way he stood there—*tall, broad, radiating Wolfy confidence and looking at me like I was something special.*

Something sacred.

Something his.

It was a look no one had ever given me before.

Certainly not Richard "Can't Take a Hint" Daniels, who somehow managed to slither back towards me.

And I think he was still flapping his gums too.

Like a petulant child whining for a treat.

"Evelyn? I'm talking to you. I demand to know who this man is! Who the heck do you think you are?" Dick demanded, puffing out his chest like a peacock with a stubby wand and unresolved mother issues.

"I'm the guy you probably don't wanna test right

now, pal. Or better yet, go ahead," Jaxson said calmly, folding his arms over his chest.

His arms.

Good Gaia, those arms.

His sleeves strained over thick biceps like the fabric was begging for mercy.

He had the kind of body that made a girl want to commit sins just by imagining the word *plaid*.

I blinked. Focus, Evie.

Richard sputtered.

"Excuse me? I am a decorated Fire Chief, thank you very much."

"Decorated?" I scoffed. "With what? Glitter glue and a participation trophy for Most Likely to Mismanage a Magical Emergency?"

Jaxson smirked, clearly enjoying my sass.

"Evelyn, I think we should discuss our business privately and leave this *person* out of it."

"Are you serious? Dick, I think you should get out of my face. Like now," I said, narrowing my eyes at Jaxson's stupid sexy grin.

It wasn't fair for one person to have a smile that freaking hot.

And the bastard knew he looked good doing it, didn't he? Of freaking course, he did.

His face should be illegal.

Especially his eyes.

Stardust, I'd called them.

He really did sparkle. Freaking stupid, smug supernatural menace.

"I believe the lady asked you to move along," Jaxson said with the same terrifying calm. "So how about you do that, and we don't have to turn this cemetery into a dueling ground?"

"Evie," Dick whined, sounding exactly like the kind of man who still lived in his mother's basement. "You're just going to let some mangy mutt talk to me like that?"

"Mangy mutt?" Jaxson echoed. His voice was velvet and violence wrapped in bourbon.

"Evie Darlin', you got about ten seconds to tell me not to bury this man where he stands."

Oh. Oh no.

And oh yes.

I should have stopped him.

Should have done something mayoral.

But instead?

I cackled.

Like full-on, ugly belly laughed in the middle of the damn cemetery, while my ex turned an interesting shade of puce and my maybe-mate cracked his knuckles in anticipation.

It wasn't my most professional moment, but in my defense, I'd had quite the week.

"I'm fine, Jaxson," I finally managed, once I wiped the tears from my eyes. "But I appreciate the enthusiasm."

"If you say so, Darlin'. But if you ever change your mind."

His expression shifted, and there it was again—that heat.

That possession.

The look that said you're mine without ever needing words.

Dick scoffed. "Ugh, whatever. You two deserve each other."

"Damn straight, we do," Jaxson murmured, not taking his eyes off me for a second.

Dick stomped off in a huff, probably to go haunt someone else's morning, and I was left standing there with six feet of smoldering Wolf Shifter and a whole lot of unsaid things between us.

"So," I said, smoothing down my shirt that was suddenly too hot and too tight. "You just happened to be wandering through my graveyard this morning?"

He didn't smile. Not exactly.

But his mouth curled up at the corners in a way that made my knees wobble.

"Couldn't stay away," he said. "You were in my dreams, Darlin'. Screaming my name. You sure you didn't feel it? I thought you had a little *Seer* in you?"

"If I do," I said dryly, "she's just as confused as the rest of me."

He took a slow step forward, and Gaia help me, I didn't back away.

"Guess I'll have to help you figure it out then."

My breath caught.

This day was shaping up, and it was still early.

Jaxson invaded my space.

His lemon-basil growly goodness was making me tremble where I stood.

"So, where to, Madam Mayor?"

"Oh, um, this way," I muttered, and turned around, but not before I saw the way his eyes smoldered as he raked them down my body.

Yep. Friday was already kicking Thursday's ass.

CHAPTER TEN—EVIE

OKAY, so by this time, I was half convinced my brain had turned to fondue.

Not the fancy kind with wine and nutmeg either —just straight up, melted, ooey-gooey mess thanks to one too-hot-for-my-sanity Werewolf walking at my side.

As we crested the gentle slope toward the Castorini Mausoleum, the moldy, sour scent that had started as a whiff turned into an aggressive slap to the nostrils.

Something was definitely off. Cemeteries had their own bouquet—*earthy, musty, vaguely funereal*—but this? This was wrong.

Like something had been disturbed.

Or pissed off.

Or both.

"You smell that?" I asked, already knowing the answer.

I could practically taste it.

And no one wants to taste ghost stink just after the ass crack of dawn on a Friday.

"I do smell that," Jaxson said, his voice low and rumbling like distant thunder.

He stepped beside me again, protective instincts flaring like neon. He filled his lungs, expelling them with a deep rumble.

"It ain't natural."

"Tell me about it," I murmured, but I wasn't sure if I meant the atmosphere or my stupid reaction to him.

Can you say new underwear stat?

I pressed my palm flat to the stone façade of the crypt, letting my magic seep out, coaxing the building to give up its secrets.

Most people thought talking to the dead was all candlelight, Latin chants, and the occasional floating table.

But for me, it was more like sticking my finger into a haunted electrical socket and hoping I didn't get zapped into another plane of existence.

A shiver ran up my spine.

My breath fogged in front of me.

In early September.

In Jersey.

Yup, definitely ghost stuff.

"I'm going to try to make contact," I whispered.

"Contact with who?"

"I dunno yet. Hopefully, someone not in a vengeful mood."

Jaxson said nothing, but I heard the unmistakable sound of claws unsheathing.

He was ready to rip into something, should it decide to float my way with bad intentions.

Strangely, that gave me comfort.

It was kind of like showing up to a knife fight with a tank wearing Levi's.

I closed my eyes and let the hum of the earth settle under my feet.

A pale shimmer of light pulsed beneath my fingertips as the spell activated.

Images flickered behind my eyelids.

A boy's scream.

Scraping.

Something *dragging?*

I gasped and pulled my hand back.

"Evie?" Jaxson stepped in close, warm and solid, one hand hovering just above the small of my back.

He didn't touch me, not quite, but the heat of him curled around me like a blanket made of bourbon, smoke, and lemon-basil goodness.

"It's not just a prank," I said slowly. "Something is haunting the cemetery. I saw, I think I saw a kid, and something chasing him. But I couldn't see what. The image cut off."

Jaxson's eyes went silver-bright, glowing faintly even in the weak morning light.

"You sure you're alright?" he asked, voice softer now.

Concerned. Protective.

"I'm fine," I lied.

The truth was, my knees were wobbly, my magic was tingling uncomfortably beneath my skin like ants on espresso, and I was way too aware of the Shifter beside me.

But I wasn't about to admit any of that.

Mayor Evie Castor did not swoon over hot strangers in cemeteries while doing her civic duty, thank you very much.

"Well, you say fine, but I can smell a lie, Darlin'," Jaxson drawled.

"You can? Dammit," I muttered.

"Besides, your aura's twitchin' somethin' fierce."

I blinked. "Excuse me?"

He smiled, slow and sinful.

"My mama taught me to read magic in a woman the way some men read poker hands. And, Sugar, yours is a five-alarm fire right now."

Oh. My. Gaia.

I was going to die.

Not from ghost attacks.

From embarrassment.

Spontaneous combustion by flirtation.

That's how Evie Castor would go down in the books.

"I'm not twitching," I snapped, patting down my curls that were definitely frizzing out under the strain of this moment. "I'm perfectly composed. Mayor-like. Regal, even."

Jaxson leaned down and murmured in my ear, "Sure you are, Darlin'. But if you ever want help smoothing out those sparks, I got just the touch."

I choked on my own saliva.

Mortifying.

And then he winked.

He freaking winked.

Why do men always have the best damn eyelashes? Jaxson's were thick and long, inky black and sexy as fuck.

Ink swirled across his skin, from what I could see of his arms and neck.

His shaggy hair was pulled back in a ponytail that made him look hotter than Aunt Edna's *Shrimp Fra Diavolo* recipe.

If I didn't stop staring like right now, I was gonna jump him.

"Let's focus on the haunting," I managed to croak out. "If something's loose in this graveyard, it's my job to contain it. Not flirt it into submission."

He held up his hands. "You got it, Madam Mayor. You lead. I'll just be your backup."

The way he said backup made me think of all sorts of unholy things—*none of which involved ecto-plasm or city paperwork.*

But I pulled myself together.

Somehow. I straightened my spine, marched toward the mausoleum's cracked door, and pretended my thighs weren't trying to start a drum line just from being in his orbit.

If the ghosts didn't kill me, my libido definitely would.

The name *Castorini* was etched across a slab of old-world Italian marble, imported straight from my great-great-grandfather's birthplace just outside Naples.

Our family mausoleum was, *well*, impressive.

Statuesque. A bit foreboding.

Okay, fine, it gave me the heebie-jeebies and smelled like the inside of an old spellbook that hadn't been opened in a few centuries.

Vittorio Alfonso Guglielmo Castorini—*try saying that five times fast with a mouthful of cannoli*—was the first of our line to cross the Atlantic.

He came over in the 1700s along with a whole flotilla of supernatural immigrants looking for better covens, less stake-burning, and more access to pizza. (I assume.)

Eventually, Castorini got shortened to *Castor*, and when dear old Nonno founded this quirky little magical hamlet, the grateful locals named it after him.

Which sounds sweet until you remember that supernatural towns don't name themselves after *nice* Wizards.

They name themselves after powerful ones.

Powerfully unpredictable ones.

He died long before I was born, as did his son.

But his grandson—*my grandfather*—now that was another story.

My gaze drifted to the engraved nameplate of Alfonso Castor.

Grandpa Al.

The one who used to bring me fresh pineapples and call me pretty even when I was covered in Nonna's marinara from head to toe.

He'd pinch my cheeks so hard I'd need a healing balm, but I'd loved him, anyway.

He was warm.

Funny.

Always smelled like tobacco, sugar, and old magic.

Then, one day, *poof.*

Gone.

No warning.

No goodbye.

Just vanished like a fart in the wind.

I stepped closer, squinting at the plaque bearing his name. Something flickered.

A strange, viscous shimmer coated the stone like ghostly snail slime—*and I didn't need a spellbook to tell me it was the bad kind of magic.*

Putrid green and faintly glowing.

Yup. That was never a good sign.

Jaxson took one long inhale beside me and grimaced. "Smells like rot."

"Yeah, well, it shouldn't," I muttered. "Mausoleums are sealed with anti-decay wards. This place is supposed to be magically protected from anything decomposing or demonic. Or both."

We lingered in tense silence, our boots crunching over wet grass and wilted offerings as the air grew colder—still.

It was that creepy sort of silence that makes even the bravest Witch hesitate. But whoever or *whatever* had spooked the kids? It was gone. For now.

"Looks like the spook's cleared out," Jaxson said after another careful look around.

I sighed, already glancing at my phone. "Yeah, and I have a job to do."

And, Gaia help me, I wanted to stay—either to chase down the magical disturbance or to keep staring at this stupidly hot Werewolf like he was the last cinnamon roll at brunch.

I wasn't sure which motive was stronger, which probably said a lot about my current mental health.

But I couldn't stay.

Responsibility called.

So I turned to go.

"Evie," he said, and I paused—just like that. One word from his lips, and I halted.

Like I was under a binding charm.

Smooth. Real smooth.

He caught up in three easy steps, all long legs and

slow-burning charm wrapped in a cotton shirt and sinfully snug jeans.

I tried to keep my eyes on his *face,* I swear.

"The boys and I were wonderin' if there's a place we can stay around here that's more comfortable than our broken down truck or the woods?" he asked, voice warm as whiskey.

"A motel? Boarding house? Somewhere we can rest our heads while the truck's gettin' fixed."

"Oh, um, yeah! Actually there is. Maribella—*she runs The Tasty Tart, you met her*—has a little cottage behind the bakery she rents out sometimes. Just tell her I sent you."

"Appreciate it, Darlin'," he said, stepping a little closer.

Close enough for his scent to roll over me again, lemon and basil and male.

Then he reached out and touched my hair.

I froze.

"What are you doing?" I asked, but I didn't move.

Couldn't.

My boots were rooted to the mossy ground as if I'd been hit by a magical bear trap.

"Couldn't help myself, Pretty Girl," he murmured, brushing his fingers down the freshly styled strands Donatella had tamed for me that morning. "You do your hair just for me?"

"Um, yeah. I mean, no. No! Not for you. For me. Obviously," I babbled, heat rushing up my cheeks so fast I probably looked like a tomato at a farmer's market.

Because who was this man, and why did his compliments land like full-body enchantments?

He was too much. Gorgeous, growly, Southern manners, and now *attentive*?

Nope. Nope.

This was a trap alright.

A handsome, muscled, flirty Werewolf trap.

And I was the dumb little bunny hopping right into the snare.

Still, I didn't trust myself to speak. Not yet anyway.

CHAPTER ELEVEN-JAXSON

STALKING the curvy little brown-haired Witch to the cemetery this morning was easy as pie.

Too damn easy, if I'm being honest.

Woman wouldn't last five minutes out in the wilds of Shifter territory with that level of obliviousness.

I made a mental note to work with her on situational awareness—*right after I convinced her to let me stay within pouncing distance.*

But gods above and below, I didn't mind the view.

Not one bit.

That swing in her hips? Hypnotic.

The kind of sway that made a man forget his name, his rank, his reason for drawing breath.

She wore these bright, ridiculous orange pants that hugged her in all the right ways, like the universe had stitched them just for her curves.

And that wild brown mane of hair—freshly styled, I might add—bounced with every step like it had its own brand of magic.

I itched to tangle my fingers in it. Just once. Or a hundred times.

I told myself I was just making sure she got to work safely.

That's it. That was the plan.

But then I saw him—that rat-faced, overconfident, pants-too-tight Wizard trying to cozy up beside her.

Dick.

No really, that was his actual name.

And honestly, it fit.

My hands curled into fists before I even realized it.

My Wolf didn't like him.

Not just because the guy was annoying.

Not even because he was clearly an ex.

It was because he had the gall to stand that close to my mate.

The fact that Evie didn't hex him into next week

immediately was a testament to her restraint—or maybe she was just too nice.

But I wasn't.

I stepped out from the trees before my Wolf could take over and do something permanent.

I figured I'd let her decide how we handled it.

If she wanted him gone, I'd do it without leaving a mark.

Okay, maybe one small mark.

But she gave me a look. One of those warning looks women are born knowing how to make. So I backed off. For now.

Didn't mean I liked it.

My Wolf was pacing inside me like a caged thing.

He'd already marked her scent, memorized the sound of her voice, the pulse beneath her skin, the exact tilt of her head when she got annoyed.

She was his. Mine. Ours.

Dual-natured creatures such as myself often had a difficult time separating the two aspects of our personality.

Sometimes—*like with me*—our animal halves seemed to have minds of their own.

Just so happened that my Wolf and I agreed vehemently on this one particular thing.

Mainly, Evelyn Castor was mine. Ours. Whatever.

Point was, that idiot Wizard? He was out of the picture, Permanently.

And if he knew what was good for him, he'd better take the hint and stay gone.

After that little tête-à-tête, I tried to focus on the cemetery.

The stench of rot clinging to the air wasn't natural—and the sickly green magic smeared across her family's mausoleum? That was even worse.

I didn't need my years as a firefighter, or my time wearing a badge back in Rottingham County, Texas, to know something was seriously off.

Some things you just feel in your bones—and this? This reeked of trouble.

The protective wards on that place were old magic, and whatever tainted it wasn't friendly.

But even as I sniffed the air and scanned for signs of movement, my damn brain kept short-circuiting back to her.

My curvy Witch mate.

Unclaimed, yes. But mine all the same.

The way her brows furrowed when she was concentrating.

The way she stood her ground even when she was clearly freaked out.

The way she rolled her eyes at me like I was a walking inconvenience, while her heartbeat betrayed her interest.

She didn't know what she meant to me yet.

Didn't know how my blood sang for her, how my magic was already syncing up with hers like gravity finding its pull.

Evie Castor didn't believe in fate, I could tell that much.

She'd been burned.

Once, maybe more.

And now she wore her independence like armor.

But armor didn't scare me.

I had claws that could peel it back, and a heart that beat only for her.

I wasn't going anywhere. Not until she saw what I saw.

Not until she knew that she was everything I needed.

And I planned to spend every second proving it.

One date. One taste. That's all I needed to start.

After that?

She'd never want to walk through this town

alone again. Not when she could have me by her side —*her partner, her protector, her mate.*

And gods help the next Wizard who tried to test me.

Because next time? I wouldn't be so damn polite.

"Well, that concludes all the time I have for investigating right now," she said, and I nodded, following her out.

"What are you doing?" she asked as I continued to walk beside her.

"I'd think that was obvious," I replied, and grinned at her cute portrayal of annoyance.

Truth was I needed a moment to collect my thoughts.

I had a question for Evie. A big question, and it was far more personal and important than anything I'd ever asked a woman before.

Nerves the likes of which I've never experienced filled me.

Would it be too much to ask her out already?

Maybe.

But I've never been the type to wait around once I know what I want.

And I wanted Evie Castor.

She wasn't just some pretty face. She was *it*. No doubt about it.

This morning only solidified what I knew. The moment I saw her—*bossing around ghosts and ex-boyfriends with one bloodshot eye and enough attitude to floor a grown man*—I was gone.

Hooked. Head over tail.

Now she was turning to leave, those hips swaying in those ridiculous orange pants, and all I could think about was how I was gonna make her mine.

Slowly, surely, and the right way.

"Would it be too forward if I asked you out on a date tonight?" I asked, keeping it light.

Letting the drawl roll off my tongue like honey. She stiffened for a second.

Paused. Turned back to me with one eyebrow raised sky high and those big brown eyes wide as can be.

Bingo. Got her attention.

She glanced back at me, lips parting like she wasn't sure whether to laugh or hex me.

"Is that really a good idea? I mean, you aren't staying here long."

I let a slow smile spread across my face.

Damn, she was cute when she tried to play it cool. Like I couldn't see the spark in her eyes or smell the desire rolling off her in waves.

"Maybe," I said, stepping closer, just enough to

see the pulse flutter at her throat. "But we gotta eat, right? Does seven suit you?"

She hesitated again, just for a beat.

Then, she said, "Yeah. I can be ready at seven."

"Perfect," I said, and before my better judgment kicked in, I leaned in and kissed her.

Just a quick taste. A whisper of a claim.

Her lips were soft and warm and tasted faintly of cinnamon and sass.

Gods, I wanted more.

But I backed off, tucking my hands in my back pockets before they wandered to places that would definitely get me banned from the town before dinner.

She just stood there, staring at me like I'd short-circuited her brain.

Her cheeks flushed that pretty pink, her mouth slightly parted like she wanted to say something but forgot how to speak.

Good.

Let her feel that spark.

Let her *remember* it.

I bit my lip, holding back the full grin threatening to crack my face.

She looked like she wasn't sure whether to run, punch me, or kiss me again.

Maybe all three.

I could work with that.

But I knew I had something else to fix. And I was of a mind to get it done soon.

See, here's the thing—Evie thought I was just passing through.

That I was gonna grab dinner, maybe steal a kiss or two, and hit the road.

But nah. She couldn't be more wrong.

I was staying. Right here. In Castor's Corner.

She didn't know it yet, but I had every intention of showing her exactly what kind of mate I could be.

Protective. Patient. Persistent.

And yeah, I had plans.

Plans to feed her. Laugh with her. Worship her body with my mouth until she forgot whatever dumbass reasons she had for pushing me away.

Plans to make her mine. *Forever.*

Let her think it's just dinner. Just a maybe.

I'll make damn sure it turns into everything.

CHAPTER TWELVE-EVIE

THE CACOPHONY of angry voices in my waiting room told me two things.

First, the townspeople had definitely heard about our new visitors.

Second, they were absolutely, unequivocally pissed off.

"Madam Mayor!"

"Evie!"

"Evelyn Castor, you must get rid of those Shifters!"

Ugh.

The name *Evelyn* being flung at me like a curse was never a good sign.

"There you are!" Stanley cried, popping his magnificently styled head into the hallway like a glamorous meerkat.

"Okay, folks, you know the drill! Fill out a form, and I will personally deliver your grievances to the mayor!"

My knight in shining purple silk Armani opened my office door and practically body-blocked me inside.

"It's about time," he hissed, giving me the once-over.

Then he turned to the crowd and clapped his hands, his tone transforming into that of an exhausted Broadway stage manager.

"Forms in the inbox, people! This is not a Witch hunt—yet!"

"I stopped by the cemetery to check on Miss Spritely's complaint," I said, brushing past him.

He gasped—like, hand-to-chest, dramatic gasp. "Ooh! What did you find? Possibly a dinner date with tall, dark, and howly?"

He waggled his brows like a villain in a sexy soap opera.

"Also, I see Donny stopped by, didn't she? Your hair is giving mid-century siren realness."

I froze mid-purse-drop. "How do you already know about Jaxson?"

Stanley perched on the corner of my desk with the balance of a dancer and the smug satisfaction of someone who read every gossip thread in town.

"Ooooh, so it *is* Jaxson, huh? That's his name? Tell me everything. Every. Sultry. Detail."

"There's nothing to tell," I said, lying like the worst liar in the history of ever. "Yet," I added, because I couldn't help myself—*and winked.*

My stomach growled in protest, which prompted me to dive for the snack drawer like a woman on a mission.

I bypassed the judgmental bags of kale chips and raw almonds in favor of something that might actually make me happy.

Like chocolate.

Or chocolate-covered chocolate.

Stanley made a noise that sounded like a dying peacock.

"Absolutely not, Evelyn Castor."

And the rat took my bar!

That was it. If he wanted to play dirty, I could play dirty.

"Really, Stanley *Moncrief?* Should we inspect your snack drawer? Maybe tell Stephen that someone hasn't given up peanut butter out of respect for his husband's food allergies, after all?"

He narrowed his eyes, then handed me a dark

chocolate granola bar like it was an offering from the gods.

I squinted at it.

"Ugh. Why am I even fighting for this? It looks like it was made by a sadist who hates joy."

He pointed dramatically to the framed photo on my desk of my mother and Aunt Edna, both beaming like Witches who had survived a thousand Weight Watchers meetings. Which they had. But I couldn't say the same for any of the others.

"Fine," I muttered, unwrapping the bar and taking a bite.

"Also? About damn time," he said, tapping one perfectly manicured finger on the wood. "After Chief Dick—"

I snorted mid-chew and nearly lost all oxygen.

I couldn't even pretend not to laugh.

And okay, *maybe* I'd let it slip one night—after a few glasses of plum wine—that Richard Daniels preferred to be called *Chief Dick* in bed.

Not that he earned the title.

His *firehose*? More like a busted sprinkler.

Jaxson, on the other hand—now that man had potential written all over him.

Oh, Gaia. Just thinking about the size of those hands gave me shivers.

"Okay, now let's be honest," Stanley continued, completely unbothered. "Shifters? *Fun size or full size?*"

He raised both index fingers and held them apart until they formed a generous, and frankly alarming, thirteen-inch gap.

I choked.

On the granola bar. Or the proposed inches.

I wasn't sure.

"Why the fuck is this so dry?" I croaked, eyes watering as I reached for his fancy bottle of imported Japanese spring water.

He let me drink it. Begrudgingly. But I knew it hurt him.

Once I swallowed the desert masquerading as a granola bar, I leaned back in my chair.

"Thanks, Stan. I know it's not permanent or anything. But I am *really* attracted to this guy."

Stanley softened. "Evie, babe, you have the Sight. You can see ghosts. You can ferret out lies. You even predicted Mrs. Wendell's cat would return—and it did, with kittens."

"I still think that was a hallucination," I muttered.

"But you *can't* read your own future, and that's okay," he said gently. "Don't overthink it. Don't worry about it. Worrying gives you wrinkles and gray hairs. Just boink the guy and enjoy it!"

"And hexing the town's water supply would get me fired," I added, then gasped. "Boink the guy? Really?"

Stanley just patted my hand.

"Oh! By the way, you had a phone call," he said casually.

"From who?" I asked, brows shooting up.

He filtered every message like a spellbound gate-keeper. If he was mentioning one? It was serious.

Please don't be my parents.

Please don't be my parents.

Please don't be my parents.

I could not deal with one more honeymoon story.

Seriously, I was seconds away from banishing myself to another realm if my dad said one more thing about *seducing my mother under the crescent moon.*

Yuck. Gross. Barf.

Apparently, all Castor Witches had overactive gag reflexes.

It was genetic.

"Now, don't get your panties in a twist," Stanley said, sweeping into the room with the confidence of a runway model and the sass of a drag queen at brunch. "But I thought you'd want to hear this from me directly."

He paused just long enough to make me nervous. "She called to check in today. Mentioned a few things. Oh, and it seems our fabulous town Witch Trifecta has been criminally lax about selecting familiars. She's sending three—*immediately*. They've read your files. And she casually mentioned a few Shifters might've wandered into the area and with her full approval."

Wait.

What? Who?

The fuck?

My heart hiccupped. My magic stirred.

Stanley kept talking, oblivious to the existential spiral forming in my brain.

"She called about eight seconds before Dick Daniels barged in here, foaming at the mouth, ranting about a 'Shifter menace threatening our supernatural way of life.' You know. Typical Dick behavior."

"Ugh. Screw Dick," I muttered, my pulse ticking upward. "But Stanley—you keep saying she. Who is *she*?"

There was only one *she* that could make my

stomach plummet and my mouth go dry like I'd swallowed a sand dune.

Stanley just smiled. That smile. The evil one he reserved for when he was about to drop a bomb and then leave me to clean up the magical fallout.

"Stanley," I warned.

"Yep," he sang.

I took a sip of water just as he added, "Magdelena called."

Cue spit-take.

Right onto his custom Armani.

Oops.

Sorry not sorry.

"Evelyn!" he shrieked, magicking away the stain.

"You mean Magdelena?" I gasped. "Like the Magdelena? La Befana? The Witch Whisperer?!"

"She prefers Witch Wheedler, but yes." Stanley plucked a lint roller from his drawer and cleaned a speck that wasn't there, more offended by my manners than my spit.

"I am not calling her that," I said.

Then, I jumped up, then sat back down, then stood again before remembering how knees work.

"Holy crap. Why would she call me?!"

"I just told you why," Stanley repeated, rolling his eyes.

"Number," I barked. "Give me her number!"

He sauntered—*yes, sauntered*—across the room like he had all the time in the world.

Finally, his neon green notepad floated into my hand.

"Stanley, what even is this handwriting? It looks like magical hieroglyphics."

"It's calligraphy, and it's elevated," he sniffed. "That's a five, not an S, you philistine."

"Sorry. Thank you. I love your art. Culture is life. Okay, I got this. Let me call this, um, *legend* before I explode."

He rolled his eyes but gave me a thumbs up.

I dialed with shaking fingers and prayed to the goddess I wouldn't puke. When the line clicked, a raspy voice that could only belong to a thousand-year-old badass came through.

"Hello! You've reached the mighty Shifter Wheedler! Hello? Is this thing on? Hurry up, sister, I ain't got all day!"

Oh my gods, it's her.

"Magdelena?!" I squeaked like a baby squirrel with a megaphone.

"Speaking. Hang on." She covered the phone, I think, because I heard something that sounded like whispering, a scuffle, a chair squeak, and possibly someone being smacked on the ass.

I stared at Stanley, who was now pacing, gesturing wildly for updates like I was giving a TED Talk instead of peeing my pants mid-call.

Then she was back.

"Alright. So. What can I do you for?" she said, now sounding like a twenty year-old, and acting like she hadn't just had a whole three-ring circus going on wherever she was.

"This is Evie Castor of Castor's Corner, just returning your call," I said, trying not to squeak again.

"Castor's what now? Wait—Efraim?" she shouted.

"It's Evie," I corrected.

"Sure it is," she replied distractedly. I heard more shuffling, maybe a thud.

Definitely a moan. Was she working right now or filming a porno?

Finally, she returned, clear as a bell.

"Of course, Evie, doll. So, it's come to my attention, via the holy offices of the Mystical Magical Morrigan herself, that the Witch Trifecta of your adorable little hamlet has been without familiars for some time now."

"Uh, yeah. The last Trifecta lost their familiars in that unfortunate incident involving those rogue warlocks, a bonfire, and half of Main Street, so we just thought it would be better," I winced, trying to explain.

"Well, sweetheart, that dog won't hunt anymore," she snapped. "I've got three familiars incoming to your sweet little town of Cassius Clay—wait, is that in Joizy?"

"No one says Joizy," I muttered.

"Whatevah," she replied, nailing the accent in a way that both enraged and impressed me.

I grinned despite myself. "So these familiars, are they mandatory?"

"Mandatory. Obligatory. Call it whatevah you want. But, uh, so yeah, don't freak out, but they're a little *unconventional*. Oh, and I let them read your files and choose their own Witches themselves. Sounded fair."

"Wait, our files?"

"Yep. The Mighty Morphin Power Morrigan has files on everybody. Let's see—Evelyn Castor, Maribella Strega, and Donatella Andrews. Your girl squad is about to get a triple dose of magical companionship."

Familiars. Shifters.

La Befana sending us backup in three tiny, fragile, furry forms.

Well, crap.

My brain short-circuited.

My hormones were still trying to get over Jaxson's smile.

"Every Witch needs a familiar, even Witches in Catsup Cottage."

"Castor's Corner," I mumbled.

"You know your tiny town is prophesied to do big things for the magical world! Big things."

I had an actual legend on speed dial and a prophecy unfolding before breakfast?

I reached for Stanley's water again.

Yep. I was gonna need a real snack—*the buttery, warm from the oven, gooey-filled kind.*

And possibly a nap.

And definitely some wine.

CHAPTER THIRTEEN—EVIE

DID I mention I never liked the idea of having a familiar?

Yeah. Never.

Not once in my entire life had I yearned for a magical sidekick, companion, or spirit animal.

I didn't want something fluffy and mysterious following me around, purring judgment or critiquing my dating life.

Or worse—offering unsolicited advice in rhyme.

Ugh. No, thank you.

"Is it a bad time to mention a cat allergy?" I asked, trying for casual. Not for a friend.

"No worries, these guys are not felines," Magdelena replied breezily. "Anywho, they'll arrive within the next twenty-four hours, and I expect the three of you to properly welcome them, *capisce?*"

Of course, her pronunciation was deplorable. Came out more like *"ca-pissy,"* but I did not dare correct her.

I valued my limbs and my standing in the coven hierarchy too much.

"Uh, yep. Got it." I winced.

"Next on my list for Candida Caverns is—oh yeah, crap, I see you guys have some bad juju going on. You okay to nip that in the bud?"

"Candida? Did you just call our town yeast infection caverns?" I blurted before my brain could catch up to my mouth.

"What was that?" she asked, clearly distracted.

"Nothing." I coughed. "Um, bad juju? Oh! You mean the cemetery sightings. Yes, I'm on it."

"Great," she said, humming something vaguely disco-inspired and completely off-key.

"Uh, anything else?" I asked, trying to keep my voice neutral.

The humming was grating, but you didn't rush a Witch like Magdelena.

That was how you ended up cursed into an office chair or turned into a potted plant.

"Yes, one more thing for Caboodle Circle."

"Castor's Corner," I mumbled through gritted teeth for the umpteenth time.

"That's what I said. Oh, yeah—my significant other, the Wizard Wonder, also known as Orpheus Ladonia, the hot dad-body-rockin' sex machine I'm mated to—informed me you've got three new supes in town."

"Yes. They arrived yesterday," I confirmed, cheeks heating at the thought of Jaxson and his unfairly perfect everything.

"Cool. Well, from what I've gathered they were supposed to be on their way to Maccon City but got sidetracked. I understand their car is being fixed, and they'd like to stay a few days in Cameron's Clover. Is that going to be a problem?"

"No, of course not," I lied. "Castor's Corner is happy to have them."

And yes, I cringed at the blatant falsehood.

Of course it was going to be a problem.

For several reasons!

One, this was Cameron's Clover—fuck, I meant Castor's Corner.

Outsiders always caused chaos here, like that time a fae wedding accidentally triggered a dimension rift in the middle of a dog grooming competition.

Two, I had zero idea how I was going to get through dinner tonight without climbing Jaxson like a tree and marking him like a territorial tomcat.

Three, and this was a big one, once I jumped him—I was fairly certain I wouldn't want to let him go.

I got possessive with lovers. And Jaxson? He smelled like home and lemon bars.

There was no coming back from that.

And four, I still hadn't figured out what kind of malicious magical crap was oozing green rot all over my family mausoleum.

So yeah.

Big problem.

"Alrighty then, toodles!" Magdelena screeched into the phone, followed by a click.

I sat there blinking, still holding the receiver to my ear like a moron, as if the sound waves might offer a clue about what just happened.

Spoiler alert: they didn't.

I doubted a trained psychiatrist could make sense of the hot mess that was that phone call.

How the hell was I supposed to?

"Well?" Stanley asked, hands on his hips and looking way too smug for a man who'd just been spit on with designer water.

I opened my mouth to answer—but before I could, someone knocked on the office door.

"I got it," Stanley muttered, striding over like he was about to personally cast out a demon.

He flung the door open, and the moment he gasped, I knew I was in for it.

"You Evie?" a voice rumbled.

Low. Gravelly. Thick with an accent that gave me chills in a *I've seen too many dark European thrillers* kind of way.

The sound of it reminded me of those Peter Bebjak films they played at the Castor's Corner Indie Theater every Friday night.

Yes, we had culture.

And yes, I adored a good Slovak horror film with subtitles and blood magic.

I heard something skitter.

A clicking sound—sharp and close.

I leaned over my desk, trying to see past my overflowing inbox and oversized monitor, but my legs had suddenly lost all motivation to stand.

"I stutter?" the voice snapped again.

And that's when I realized *the familiars had arrived.*

And they were not cute little cats in bows or elegant owls with scrolls.

Oh, no.

My familiar had an accent, an attitude, and a terrifying ability to make Stanley, the most unflappable man I knew, pale five shades lighter.

Goddess, help me.

This was going to get weird. Real fast.

Stanley shook his head slowly, chin practically touching his chest as he pointed a trembling finger in my direction. Odd.

The man was rarely rendered speechless.

Appalled? Yes.

Sarcastic? Always.

But speechless? Almost never.

"Evelyn Castor?" the creature said, in a voice that could make bricks shiver.

He was holding a manila envelope in a clawed hand that looked like it had snatched a few souls in its day.

I swallowed hard and stood up, feeling that weird little zing in my gut that warned me magical nonsense was afoot.

The *being* who had spoken was about two and a half feet tall and standing upright like a tiny professor about to give me a lecture on proper summoning etiquette.

Two more stood flanking him, looking just as strange—*and just as unimpressed.*

They had shaggy fur in black, gray, and white, like some goth Muppet makeover gone awry.

Their enormous eyes glowed faintly, almost otherworldly, and each had a pair of horns jutting out from their heads at odd, slightly sinister angles.

Oh, and tails.

Long, ropy tails that curled behind them like mischievous punctuation marks.

"Yep. That's me. Call me Evie," I said cautiously. "You guys the familiars?"

Three nods.

Simultaneous. Precise.

A little unnerving, honestly.

"Cool. Hold that thought." I grabbed my phone and sent a text with the urgency of a woman about to be left alone with magical raccoons who could probably curse my entire bloodline.

ME

Get your asses here now. And I mean NOW.

I looked back up and found one of them—*gray-furred and slightly taller than the others*—eyeing me with what could only be described as disapproval.

"Where are the other Trifecta Witches?" he asked, same thick Eastern European accent.

Slovakia? Romania? Transylvania?

Honestly, he sounded like he belonged in a gritty Netflix fantasy series narrated by Liam Neeson.

"They're on their way," I replied. "Do you guys have names?"

"Of course," scoffed the shortest one, who had white fur and the most judgmental tail flick I'd ever seen.

"I am Ivan," said the envelope-holder in the middle. "This is Gryn, and this is Petyr. We are the *Domovyk*."

"The who now?"

"Domovyk," Ivan repeated. "We were once minor household gods."

"*Minor* but *mighty*," Gryn grumbled.

"Yet tragically displaced by microwaves and peanut butter," Petyr muttered, licking something off his claws. "I like this peanut butter."

"We now serve the Witch Trifecta," Ivan said, straightening his tiny spine like he was announcing something on the nightly news.

"Our pact with La Befana and the Morrigan is sealed. We protect the Witches. We serve the home. We keep the balance."

"Uh. Great. Tea?"

I wasn't trying to interrupt their tiny divine TED Talk, but the air was crackling around them, and my magic was reacting.

Literal flames were flickering at my fingertips, and I didn't want to accidentally light anyone's fur on fire. I'd never live that down.

Ivan noticed, growled something sharp in their native tongue, and the others fell silent instantly.

Then—*without a word*—they dropped to the floor in perfect unison.

Crisscross applesauce.

Like creepy, magical kindergartners waiting for snack time.

No. Nope.

I was not reading them *If You Give a Witch a Cupcake.*

Stanley, bless his silk-swathed soul, muttered, "I'll get the tea," and practically sprinted from the room like the floor was made of snakes.

The Domovyk didn't try to talk to me while he was gone.

Which, honestly, was fine.

But the weird, throaty clicks and low growls they whispered to each other while waiting?

Not fine. Not cute. Not one bit.

A minute later, the office door banged open, and Maribella barreled in, covered in flour and full of fury.

Donatella followed, dragging Jinx McAndrews—*a Mink Shifter, who actually had this cool throwback prehistoric gene that meant she turned into a two-ton rodent at will*—in by the arm. She looked mid-makeover with foil strips in her hair and what appeared to be a mixing bowl of magical hair dye sloshing around in her hands.

"Where's the fire? And *what the hell* are those things?" Donny screeched.

"Is this a prank? Is it April already?" Maribella panted, eyeing the trio like they might explode into confetti.

"Hello Jinx," I said coolly to the Shifter, ignoring the chaos around me.

"Mayor," she nodded, valiantly trying not to scream.

"What the? I mean, you couldn't call an exterminator?" Donny asked. "I was in the middle of highlighting Mrs. McAndrews' hair, Evie."

"And you couldn't tell her to wait?" I snapped back.

"No! Foil," she snapped, and Jinx practically threw the entire box of the stuff at her.

Snort.

I ignored the impulse to hex them both and cleared my throat.

"Ladies, meet our familiars."

All three Domovyk rose to their feet, each one stepping in front of one of us. Ivan took me.

Petyr stepped toward Maribella.

And Gryn, who had a distinct air of menace, stared Donny down like he already regretted this assignment.

"This is them? Good. Now we make our vow," Ivan said.

They bowed in unison and began to chant in a language that made my ears pop.

Green sparks lit the air.

The temperature in the room dropped ten degrees.

I didn't know how I knew what to do next—*how any of us knew*—but all three of us raised our right hands at the same moment, our pointer fingers extended.

The Domovyk reached out with clawed fingers, sparks flaring.

When our skin touched, magic zipped through me like a jolt of liquid fire.

Ivan's power felt warm and familiar. Like a memory I didn't know I had.

He was inspecting me, sensing me, syncing with me—and in that second, I *knew* they weren't malevolent.

They were ours.

"Any questions?" Ivan asked, letting go.

"Uh. No," I croaked.

Maribella and Donny echoed the same.

"Good. Then we leave."

"Wait—what? I thought you were our familiars now?"

"We are," he said flatly. "But you do not need us now. We will return when we are needed. Do not forget to leave us plates from your meals. Supper, breakfast, leftovers. Especially sweet things. *Very* important."

"Um, you want doggy bags?"

Ivan tilted his head.

"We are not dogs. But yes."

"Got it," I mumbled.

"Good," he nodded, satisfied.

Then—*with a loud pop! and a blinding flash of green* —they vanished.

We stood there in stunned silence for a moment.

Jinx, *er*, Mrs. McAndrews looked traumatized.

Maribella looked impressed.

Donny just looked irritated.

"Well," she muttered. "That happened."

Then, with a shrug, she collected Marylou and left. Bella followed closely behind with a promise to regroup later.

The rest of the day passed in a blur of paperwork, spell filings, and two passive-aggressive complaints from Dick about Jaxson's jeans being too tight.

As if that were a bad thing.

By the time five o'clock rolled around, I was ready to collapse.

My familiar had vanished after zapping my magic into overdrive.

I still didn't have a damn car.

I had a hot date with a Werewolf I wanted to climb like a fire pole.

And there was still something rotting beneath the town cemetery.

But hey. At least it was Friday.

CHAPTER FOURTEEN-JAXSON

I CAUGHT her just as she stepped out of City Hall, cell pressed to her ear and murder in her eyes.

She was pacing like the sidewalk had personally committed any number of heinous acts against her or her ancestors.

Damn. She was cute.

"No, I don't care if he wants a column titled *Witches Behaving Badly*. Tell Ryerson if he wants to print trash, he can do it in crayon on a napkin," she snapped. Then added with a honeyed bite, "Yes, Stanley. I do know it's his constitutional right to be an ass."

I leaned against the stone rail, a white bag in my hand, watching her unleash that fire.

Gods, she was magnificent.

Fierce. Sharp.

And so damn beautiful I felt the hunger for her like claws raking down my chest.

She turned and spotted me. Froze mid-huff.

"Jaxson."

The way she said my name?

Like she hadn't meant to.

Like she was surprised I hadn't vanished.

"Afternoon, Madam Mayor," I drawled, just to see that little twitch of her lips.

"Don't start with the *Madam Mayor* stuff. You'll give people ideas."

"I already got ideas," I said, low and honest.

Her eyes flared, cheeks going that pretty pink again.

I stepped forward, slowly, letting her see I was here for her and only her.

Then I held out the white sack. "Thought you might want something sweet to take the edge off before dinner, Darlin'."

She took it with a raised brow, peeked inside, and lit up like dawn breaking. "*Double Devil's Food Delights?*"

She inhaled and practically moaned.

And poof! There went any chance I had of taking this thing slowly.

"These are my favorite."

"I know," I said, voice rougher than I meant. "And dammit, Darlin', I've never been jealous of a pastry before."

She didn't catch it at first—too busy licking chocolate off her fingers and making soft, sinful sounds that made my jeans a damn prison.

I had to shift my stance, *subtly*, adjusting myself before she noticed.

"Huh?" she asked, blinking at me with chocolate-glazed satisfaction.

"Nothing," I muttered, fighting for control.

"So," she said, wiping her lips on the tiny napkin provided.

She was a little bit shy now.

So fucking adorable.

"What did you have in mind for dinner? Pizza? A burger?"

"I thought I'd cook for you," I said, stepping closer again. "Some food, some wine, conversation. Maybe get to know you a bit. That is, if you're amenable, Darlin'."

That pet name rolled off the tongue effortlessly. And I could tell she liked it.

It worked just like a charm—*her eyes darkened with interest, her body leaned subtly toward mine.*

Oh yeah, she felt it too.

"Sounds good," she said, then squinted. "But you, uh, have no kitchen."

"Thought I'd borrow yours."

I took her hand. She didn't pull away.

Instead, she let me hold it as we walked straight through the middle of town like we'd been doing it for years.

She asked about my opinions on local sports.

I asked about her take on country music.

We bickered over the New York Giants versus the Dallas Cowboys.

She wrinkled her nose at my playlist choices.

It was perfect.

We stopped at the market.

Best of all? She didn't let go of my hand the whole time.

"You're not a vegetarian, are you?" I asked, eyeing her sideways.

"Who me? No, I'm not a vegetarian."

"Thank the Moon," I muttered, tossing two porterhouse steaks into the basket.

Then came potatoes, broccoli, cheddar, bacon, red wine.

She didn't say a word—*just nodded like she approved of every choice.*

And when I reached for the strawberries, dark chocolate, sugar, and cream, I heard the faintest gasp.

Yeah. She knew what was coming.

By the time we got back to her place, my Wolf was pacing under my skin, eager and keyed up.

Not just for the night. For her.

"Why don't you go set your things down?" I said, voice gentler now.

"I know it might be odd, since this is your house and all, but I'd really like you to be comfortable with me, Evelyn Castor."

She tilted her head, heat in her gaze. "If I wasn't comfortable, you wouldn't have made it through the front door."

She stepped close.

Her curves brushed my chest, and I had to grit my teeth to keep my growl in check.

Lightning danced through my veins. My Wolf liked her boldness.

Hell, so did I.

"You keep looking at me like that, Darlin', and I'm liable to want my dessert right now."

"Hungry, are you?" she asked, voice low and knowing.

"Wolves are always hungry for some things."

She pressed even closer.

"What's wrong with eating dessert first?"

"Normally I'd say nothin'," I murmured, brushing my lips near hers. "Nothin' at all."

A pause, then, "Evie," I moaned, pressing my forehead against hers, just breathing her in.

I was seconds from kissing her, but boundaries and explanations had to be made.

Both were necessary because this *thing* between us?

It wasn't a *one and done*.

It was more a *till death, but maybe not even then* kind of deal.

"I think this thing between us might be bigger than we think," I growled, licked my lips, and continued, even though my Wolf was damn near tearing me up inside, "I think we should talk first."

I waited impatiently for her reply.

Then—*crash.*

The sound came from upstairs.

Evelyn jumped.

My body reacted instinctively. Protective instincts roared to life as I bolted up the stairs.

That's when I came face to face with a two-foot-tall furball crackling with green magic.

"You do not touch my Witch without permission," the creature hissed, claws lit like goddamn fireworks.

I blinked.

Evie huffed behind me.

And all I could think was, *what in the name of moonlight and madness had I just gotten myself into?*

And why did it feel like exactly where I was meant to be?

CHAPTER FIFTEEN-EVIE

I WHOLEHEARTEDLY APPROVED of every item Jaxson tossed into our cart at the market.

The steaks were thick enough to seduce a vegan.

The potatoes were large enough to make a meal on their own.

The wine?

Bold. Smooth.

Just like him.

I couldn't wait to see how he cooked everything.

But it was when he reached for the strawberries, the block of dark chocolate, the bag of powdered sugar, and the quart of heavy cream that something inside me fluttered.

No man had ever shopped for me like that before.

No one had looked at me and thought, *she needs indulgence.*

It was enough to make a girl need to change her panties.

My oh my.

By the time we made it back to my place, my whole body was buzzing with awareness.

Every glance, every brush of his arm, every smile he threw my way made it harder to remember who I was.

What I was.

That I had a town to run, a graveyard full of weirdness, a trio of familiars to manage, and a never-ending pile of bureaucratic nonsense to untangle.

But Jaxson Reid?

He was six and a half feet of sin wrapped in charm, all handholding and confidence and effortless sex appeal.

And I wanted to know everything about him.

"Why don't you go set your things down?" he said as we entered, his voice that low, dangerous growl that made me weak in the knees. "I know it might be odd, since this is your house and all, but I'd really like you to be comfortable with me, Evelyn Castor."

I turned to him, stepped into his space like it was

mine to claim. "If I wasn't comfortable, you wouldn't have made it through the front door."

His eyes darkened, silver sparks shifting to storm steel. He made a sound in his chest—a low, controlled rumble that might've been a growl or a moan, but whatever it was, it shot straight to my core.

My panties dampened even more at the sexy as sin sound.

Dinner sounded great. Really.

But I'd never been the type to eat in order.

"You keep looking at me like that, Darlin', and I'm liable to want my dessert right now."

"Hungry, are you?"

"Wolves are always hungry for some things," he murmured, eyes flashing, voice like gravel and bourbon.

I arched a brow, leaning in. "What's wrong with eating dessert first?"

"Normally, I'd say nothin' was wrong with it. Nothin' at all, Evelyn," he said, voice dipping to something downright sinful as he pulled me against the long, hard line of his body.

My knees nearly gave out.

He smelled like lemon and basil, fresh and wild

all at once, and I soaked him in like a woman starving for something more than just food.

I wanted to kiss him.

Hell, I wanted everything.

But part of me—*some deep, annoying, mayoral voice of reason*—reminded me that I wasn't just some woman.

I was Evelyn Castor. Mayor. Witch. Protector of Castor's Corner.

"Evie," he moaned, forehead resting against mine.

Gods. Just hearing my name on his lips made me ache.

It had been so long.

So damn long since I'd wanted someone like this.

In fact? I think the last time I felt this way was maybe never.

He wasn't just handsome—though, yeah, holy hell, he was.

He was *more*.

He was *patient, playful, smart, grounded.*

He'd stood by me like we belonged together.

Like I belonged to him.

And that terrified me.

Because I couldn't afford to belong to anyone.

I had a town to hold together with duct tape and stubbornness.

No time for fairytale endings or happily ever afters.

Not for me.

And when he said, "I think this thing between us might be bigger than we think," in that voice that dripped with truth and hunger, I damn near melted.

"I think we should talk first," he added, and my heart twisted.

He wanted to know me. Not just my body—*but me*.

He leaned in, lips a breath from mine then—CRASH!

A sound like a tree falling through drywall shattered the moment.

I yelped and stepped back, blinking as he snapped into protector mode and charged the stairs.

I followed, heart pounding.

"You do not touch my Witch without permission," a very hairy, very pissed off little creature hissed.

Oh shit.

Okay, my fault. I totally forgot about *him*.

Jaxson crouched low and growled, teeth bared.

And for a second, I imagined all kinds of terrible outcomes.

"Wait! This is my familiar!" I shoved between

them, hands on Jaxson's chest—which, yes, was as rock hard and glorious as I'd imagined.

Note to self: revisit that terrain later.

"You know this hairy little bugger?" he snarled, gaze flicking from me to Ivan.

"I do," I sighed. Then, I turned to the furry little menace. "Ivan, what in Gaia's name are you doing here?"

"I live here now," he grunted, clawed hand full of insulation. "Familiar, remember? *Idyot.*"

"Hey! Be nice. Now, introductions. Ivan, this is Jaxson—and by the way, he has *permission.*"

I glared at Ivan.

And I ignored the sexy Werewolf's lingering growl.

"Jaxson Reid, this is Ivan—uh, I don't know his last name," I explained.

"I am Ivan Boris Helios Godwyn Corbett Arnold Buchka Furmanovich," he said proudly.

My mouth opened. Then closed. Then opened again.

"Right. Of course you are."

Jaxson blinked. "Uh, Darlin', what exactly is he?"

I shrugged.

"My familiar. Um, Ivan here is a *domyno?* A *dominatrix?* A *Dumbledore?* A—oh, crap, I forgot."

"I am a Domovyk!" Ivan puffed up.

"Right! He's a Domovyk. That's it. A Domovyk," I said, pretending to know what that was.

"Yes. And I am *her familiar* now. You beware, Wolf man. One word and I turn your balls to green dust."

And with that, Ivan dove headfirst into the ancient dumbwaiter he'd uncovered—*because apparently that was happening now*—and disappeared with another loud crash.

Jaxson scratched his head. "Uh."

"Yeah. That went well." I covered my face.

Jaxson chuckled.

That deep, husky laugh I was quickly becoming addicted to.

I peeked through my fingers and caught a glimpse of his devil-may-care grin.

My knees wobbled.

"Come on out now, Darlin'," he whispered.

He gently peeled my hands away and framed my face with those big, calloused palms of his.

My heart slammed against my ribs.

"I was going to wait," he murmured. "But after all that, I don't think I can."

Then he kissed me.

Sweet. Deep. Unbearably tender.

It wasn't a demand—*it was a promise.*

The kind that made my soul lean in and my magic sizzle.

I moaned, melting into him, letting the kiss deepen. His lips moved with mine like we'd been kissing forever.

His tongue slid against mine, and everything else *—my town, my responsibilities, the chaos—*faded into nothing.

But I knew better.

I wasn't built for forever.

I had a town full of secrets, creatures crawling out of crypts, and a pair of best friends who barely let me pee alone, let alone date a Werewolf.

I didn't do relationships.

Just didn't have time for them.

I was Evelyn Castor.

Mayor of Castor's Corner.

Who would want that chaos for keeps?

Me—the huskily whispered word slipped into my mind before I could shut down the invasion.

Uh oh. Could it be?

CHAPTER SIXTEEN-EVIE

"WHAT DID YOU SAY?" I asked, pulling back and searching his face.

"You heard me. You just don't believe it yet."

His voice was low and steady, no trace of doubt.

He didn't smirk.

Didn't try to charm me out of my skepticism.

He just looked at me with those storm-gray eyes with flecks of lightning-silver dancing in them, quiet and sure, like he was giving me space to catch up to something he already knew.

His scent—*lemon, basil, and Wolf*—wrapped around me like a warm blanket, soothing the whirlwind in my chest.

And just when I thought I might melt right there on the floor—*grrrrooooowl.*

My traitorous stomach let out a monstrous protest, breaking the tension with all the grace of a fart at a funeral.

"That's my cue to start the grill, Darlin'," Jaxson said, and smiled like he wasn't even the slightest bit thrown.

He kissed me again—*just a taste this time, toe-curling and maddeningly brief*—then turned me toward my bedroom with a gentle swat to my generous bottom and a kiss to the back of my neck.

I sighed.

One night, I reminded myself.

I could give myself just this one night with the sexy Wolf Shifter.

But whether I was trying to keep myself from falling, or admitting I already had, I simply didn't know yet.

"Off you go, Darlin'. Go on and get yourself comfortable, then join me in the kitchen when you're ready," he whispered against my ear.

His warm citrus-scented breath made me shiver.

Not from fear.

From want.

But somehow, I managed to walk down the hall to my bedroom without tripping over my own feet.

That alone was a minor miracle.

Once inside, I shut the door behind me and leaned against it, closing my eyes.

What the frig am I doing?

I had just invited a dangerously handsome Werewolf into my home. Not just into my house—*into my space. My world. My life.*

"This is insane," I muttered to the empty room. "Take it slow? Is he kidding me? That walking fantasy of a man is making me lose my damn mind."

Yep. I was talking to myself. Full-blown muttering mess.

Mayor of a magical town and one smooth-talking Shifter had reduced me to a puddle of hormones.

I caught a glimpse of myself in the mirror and groaned.

"Good Gaia!"

What had started out as a reasonably cute outfit had been destroyed by work, stress, and a very unplanned encounter with three furballs who claimed to be ancient household gods.

My once-decent hair was now a frizzy bird's nest.

My lipstick? Gone.

My mascara? Running a marathon down my cheek.

But dammit, I wanted this night.

Wanted him.

A man—*no, a Wolf*—who cooked, smiled like he knew all my secrets and wasn't scared of any of them, and touched me like I was already his.

Twenty minutes later—after the fastest transformation of my adult life (we're talking emergency-level shower, ruthless exfoliation, tactical perfume deployment, and a full-body pep talk)—I floated down the stairs, nerves dancing in my stomach.

Okay. I *walked*. Not *floated*.

Let's not get carried away. I was in heels, not on a cloud. And unlike some Witches, I wasn't about to risk using magic to glide into a date with a smexy Werewolf. Not with the whole *no personal gain* clause hanging over my head like a magical guillotine.

Tempting the Fates? Yeah, no thanks.

Those vindictive bastards already had it out for me.

Anyway, the moment I stepped into the kitchen, I nearly stubbed my toe on my grandmother's ancient dining table.

But all was forgiven when the smell hit me.

Holy. Shit.

It was heaven.

Steaks sizzling on the grill, garlic butter melting

somewhere, roasted potatoes and cheese, bacon and red wine.

I stood in the doorway, trying not to moan out loud.

Jaxson had the back sliding door open. He had the deck all lit with fairy lights I'd strung up and promptly forgotten about.

He was out there now, looking far too good in worn jeans and a fitted tee as he turned the two beautifully seasoned steaks on the grill like he'd done it a thousand times.

I could barely breathe.

"There you are, Darlin'," he said when he turned and saw me.

He took my hand, no hesitation, just warm and steady and sure.

Usually, I hated being touched without permission.

Most men who tried it got zapped.

But not Jaxson's hands?

I wanted more.

I wanted all of him.

Every damn inch.

He led me to the outdoor table—*my mismatched silverware set out like we were at a five-star restaurant instead of my beat-up deck.*

I flushed at the sight of my chipped dishes. Really, I should have gotten them replaced ages ago, but Jaxson didn't seem to care.

He handed me a wine glass and poured generously from the bottle he'd picked out.

"Thanks," I murmured, taking a long sip.

I was going to need it.

With a wicked grin and a soft growl, my Wolfman turned back to the grill, and I let myself watch him.

Those broad shoulders.

That easy confidence.

The way his jeans hugged his—*stop.*

Focus.

After giving myself a mental shake, and pinching my thigh, I was able to answer the question he'd just asked about how I liked my meat.

"Um, medium rare, but more towards rare," I replied.

"Good girl," he said, nodding at me.

And there went the new panties I just put on.

Conversation flowed effortlessly once dinner was served, and I was shocked at how easy it was to be with him.

To laugh. To talk. To share.

"This is nice," I said, swirling my wine.

"That it is," he agreed, serving me a plate with perfectly grilled steak, loaded baked potato, and roasted broccoli.

"Now, where'd you learn to cook like this?"

"My mama," he said simply, like that explained everything.

"I appreciate a man who listens to his mama."

He grinned. "That's nice of you to say so."

Watching him eat was an *experience*.

I shouldn't have been turned on by the sight of a man biting into steak, but Gaia help me, I was.

It didn't hurt that his table manners were perfect.

No snarling.

No slobbering.

No gnawing on bones.

Not that I'd have minded. Not even a little.

"So," he said, leaning back in his chair after we both demolished our plates. "How'd you end up running this quirky little town?"

"I didn't," I admitted, stabbing a potato chunk with my fork. "The job kind of chose me."

He tilted his head, intrigued. "How's that?"

"Castor's Corner was founded by my great-grandfather. A Wizard. His wife was a Witch. They came here from Italy after some angry villagers blamed them for a bad harvest. Don't ask." I shrugged.

"Okay," he replied and grinned.

"They made a home. A sanctuary. And somewhere along the line, the town decided that each generation a living Castor heir should lead it."

"And the mausoleum? It says Castorini."

"Yeah. That was my ancestors' original surname—Castorini. Got shortened when they got here. Like a lot of immigrant names. People didn't want to learn how to spell it, so… *poof.* History rewrites itself."

I paused, suddenly self-conscious.

Not everyone got me. I knew that. And I'd grown used to the blank stares and polite nods when I got a little too passionate about lineage or lore.

But I grew up with a proud Nonna who used to scoff and say Shakespeare didn't know jack when he famously asked *what's in a name?*

According to her, everything was in a name—*roots, magic, memory.*

We Castors were taught to honor every part of our heritage.

Our name. This town.

The crazy, magical mess we came from.

Still, doubt was a sneaky bastard.

Was I rambling?

Boring him with Witchy trivia?

Drowning the mood in ancestral over sharing?

But Jaxson didn't look bored.

He didn't try to interrupt.

He just nodded thoughtfully and said, "Your Nonna sounds like a wise woman."

My breath caught. "Did I say something about her out loud?"

"No," he said softly, eyes locked on mine. "But I could hear it. Feel it."

My heart stuttered in my chest.

"You read my mind?" I whispered, voice trembling.

"No. Not your mind. Just your heart."

He reached across the table and took my hand again, thumb brushing lightly against my skin.

"How? Why?"

"You know why this is happening, Darlin'. But I'll go as slow as you need."

Fuck.

Any plans I had to be sensible flew out the window.

How the hell was I supposed to resist a man—*no, a mate*—who was that patient, that gentle, that perfect?

My nipples hardened beneath the pretty, flirty dress I'd changed into.

My sex clenched on air, heating from the inside and readying for his sweet invasion.

I licked my lips and decided to listen to my body.

"What if what I want is fast and hard?" I whispered, barely trusting my voice.

He stood, tugging me to my feet with one firm hand.

"Then I'll give it to you, Darlin'. Just as fast and hard as you want it."

And just like that, dinner was no longer the main course.

He was.

And I was starving.

Turns out, I wanted it all.

Fast and hard, yes.

But also slow and thorough.

It didn't matter.

As long as it was with him.

Only him.

Jaxson kissed me once—*deep and claiming*—before handing me my wine and turning toward the kitchen like we hadn't just been a whisper away from losing our clothes on the deck.

Everything the man did was magic.

Literal and not.

I sipped the velvety red as he cleaned up, following my instructions and leaving a small plate of supper out for Ivan like it was the most natural thing in the world.

No protest, no questions.

Just a quiet, capable strength that made my insides melt.

When he locked the screen door and turned back around, he caught me staring.

Hell, I wasn't even trying to be subtle about it.

I'd changed while he grilled—just a soft, simple button-down dress in pale plum that skimmed my curves like a spell.

No bra.

Just panties.

And beneath that flimsy bit of fabric I was just me.

Raw. Wanting. Ready.

And he could tell.

Jaxson froze for a heartbeat, eyes raking down my body with a hunger that made me tremble.

Not in fear. Never that. But anticipation.

Delicious, fluttering heat curled through my belly.

He made me feel sexy, beautiful, powerful.

Like prey who'd decided to seduce the predator.

His gaze burned into mine.

"What now?" he asked, voice low and thick.

Gravel dipped in honey.

He was giving me the choice. Putting the power in my hands.

And, Gaia help me, I wanted to use it.

"Now?" I licked my lips slowly, watching his jaw twitch. "I was hoping you knew, Wolfman."

I let my fingers trail to the top button of my dress.

His nostrils flared.

The sound that came from him was pure, unfiltered need.

A rumble, deep in his chest, vibrating with restrained hunger.

I popped the first button.

Then the second.

And the third.

No magic.

No shortcuts.

This wasn't about spells or potions.

It was about heat and trust and finally letting myself *want*.

By the time I reached the last button, the dress

fluttered open, exposing my flushed skin and soft curves to the cool kitchen air—*and to him.*

Jaxson's pupils blew wide.

His eyes darkened to storm steel and locked on my bare body like it was the only thing in the universe.

He crossed the room in two strides and stopped just short of touching me.

"Evie," he rasped, voice nearly undone.

I rose to my tiptoes and leaned in, letting my breasts graze his chest through his shirt.

"Yes, Wolfman?"

"You're playing with fire."

"Good thing I'm a Witch," I whispered, tugging his shirt from his jeans. "I know how to handle it."

He growled—*low, dangerous, and so arousing my knees nearly gave out.*

Then he was on me.

His mouth claimed mine in a kiss that could've summoned thunderstorms.

His hands were everywhere—*on my back, my hips, sliding under the fabric, lifting me like I weighed nothing.*

I wrapped my legs around his waist as he carried me to the table and laid me down like I was precious, his lips never leaving mine.

The wood was cool against my skin.

His hands were molten.

"Tell me to stop," he said against my throat, voice breaking.

"Don't you dare."

The delicious rumble coming from his chest sent spirals of pleasure straight to my girly bits.

Jaxson's eyes were back to that deep steel color that told me he was aroused.

If that wasn't evidence, then the bulge in his tight blue jeans sure as fuck was.

Looked like my Wolf was big and bad after all. Thank Gaia.

And with a flash of teeth and a groan of relief, he feasted.

Every touch.

Every kiss.

Every nip and lick felt like worship, like I was some holy offering laid out for his devotion.

He whispered things against my skin—praises, curses, promises—and I drank them in like a dying woman handed champagne.

I didn't care what he said, not really. It was the way he said it.

The heat. The reverence. The fucking hunger.

This wasn't just sex.

It was a phenomenal inevitability, our coming together.

A calling, if you will.

A storm made of heat and magic and the wild, delicious truth of who we were and what we were becoming.

I gasped as his hands gripped the sides of my panties—*what few scraps there were*—and ripped them clean off me.

Riippp. Loud and unapologetic.

Like a goddamn declaration.

"Oh, Darlin'," he drawled, rough and reverent, "look at you. So pretty and pink. You're glistening for me."

Oh. My. Goddess.

I burned under his gaze—*part shame, mostly pride.*

Because his eyes weren't mocking.

They were worshipping.

Like he'd discovered his personal holy grail and couldn't wait to dive in.

He growled again—*my name this time*—and dropped to his knees like a sinner about to get blessed.

And then he kissed me.

Right there.

On my slick, aching, ready-for-him center.

My whole body jolted like he'd plugged me into a magical generator.

His mouth was hot. His tongue was sin incarnate.

Long and wicked, it licked a slow, maddening stripe from the base of me all the way to the top, then circled my clit with a teasing flick that had me seeing actual stars.

I wasn't being poetic.

I literally gasped and saw a flash of silver behind my eyes.

"Jaxson!" I choked, voice strangled.

The man didn't answer.

He just doubled down.

He went to work, tongue fucking me like it was. His lips sucked my clit.

He made out with my pussy like he was trying to imprint his name on my soul through sheer oral devotion.

And that damn growl in his chest? Vibrated against me in the most glorious way.

I arched, fisted his thick, dark hair, and tried to hold on to something.

Sanity. My name. A single coherent thought.

Nope. All gone.

Because I wasn't Evelyn Castor anymore. I wasn't

the mayor. I wasn't the Witch who wrangled familiars, storms, and council meetings like a pro.

I was just a woman—desperate and moaning and trembling on her kitchen table while a ridiculously sexy Werewolf treated my body like a fucking delicacy.

"Fuck," I sobbed, thighs shaking, hands clutching at his shoulders like lifelines. "You're—oh Goddess—Jaxson!"

He moaned my name against me, and that was it.

I shattered.

Came so hard I thought I left my body.

My hips bucked, my toes curled, and I screamed into the universe.

His name.

Over and over again.

The orgasm rolled through me like a tidal wave, washing away all doubt, fear, and resistance.

Just gone.

It was just me, him, and the slow swirl of power crackling between our bodies.

Magic sparked in the air—*tiny, glittering flecks of light that floated up toward the ceiling like fireflies.*

When I finally opened my eyes, Jaxson was watching me with a soft, satisfied smile—*and glistening lips.*

"Holy fuck," I whispered. "What was that?"

He licked his bottom lip, slow and sinful.

"That, Darlin'? That was just dessert."

I groaned and dropped my head back against the table.

"I'm in trouble."

He leaned over me, his voice a rumble in my ear.

"You think that was trouble? 'Cause I plan to ruin you next, Madam Mayor."

Please let him be serious.

Goddess knows I wanted it.

Every second of it. *Of this.*

Him.

Me.

Us.

Together.

Finally.

CHAPTER SEVENTEEN-JAXSON

I HELPED EVIE STAND, watching with rapt attention as she let the dress fall, slow and deliberate, like a silk ribbon sliding off a gift I'd been dying to unwrap.

She stood there, completely bare, biting that plump bottom lip like she was unsure.

Like she didn't know she was the hottest damn thing I'd ever seen.

My Wolf and I were in perfect agreement.

Mine. Now. Forever.

She hesitated, a flicker of doubt in those deep brown eyes.

Did she think I'd back off?

That I'd tease and run?

Not a fucking chance.

I crossed the room in two strides and pinned her to the wall, claiming her mouth like I meant it. Because I did.

Her lips opened for me with a moan that set my entire damn body on fire.

"You sure about this?" I asked, my voice rough with need and barely held control.

"No," she whispered, her breath hot on my skin, "but let's do it anyway."

My heart slammed against my ribs at her answer.

Brave little Witch.

She had no idea what she was inviting in.

"If I take you, I won't want to give you back," I warned.

"We'll see about that," she moaned, just as my tongue found her ear and she melted into me.

Fuck.

That sound.

That scent.

She was already so soaked for me.

The taste of her coming on my mouth? Delicious.

I could still smell her arousal—*sweet and earthy with a hint of wildflowers and magic*—and it made my head spin.

My arms tightened around her as I lifted her easily and carried her up the stairs, two at a time. She clung to me, soft and warm and perfect.

I dropped her on the bed and holy hell, she jiggled.

Mine growled in approval.

"You are so beautiful, Evie Darlin'," I told her, kissing her like it was the last thing I'd ever do.

It wasn't. But it felt like it. Always would.

Mine.

She stretched under me like a cat in sunshine, licking into my mouth, tasting me.

Her body responded to my praise like I'd flipped a switch.

Goddess help me, I wanted her even more for it.

When I pulled back to strip off my clothes, her eyes flared wide.

Then she sat up and reached for me.

"Ohmygawd! You have the V!" she blurted.

"What?" I blinked, halfway out of my jeans.

"The sex lines," she said, grinning like a kid at Beltane.

I laughed, couldn't help it. Her joy was contagious.

Her fingers and lips were hot as they trailed

along my hips and down into that sweet groove that led to where I was already hard as a damn rock.

"Fuck, Darlin', you keep kissing me there and this is going to end a whole lot quicker than planned," I warned.

I felt her thoughts tumble loose.

She was trying not to think about the town, about being mayor, about the exes who walked away because she was *too much*.

But I heard it all. Felt it.

The heartbreak. The weight. The loneliness. The yearning.

You aren't too much. You're just too much for the wrong man. But not for me, Darlin'. You were made for me.

"You don't have to say it," she whispered, eyes wide. "But I hear it in your head."

"Good," I growled. "Then you know I mean every damn word."

Her hunger soared, and I caught the whisper of it —*Show me more.*

My Wolf howled at the invitation.

I surged forward and kissed her, deep and dirty, until she was gasping into my mouth.

While I had her good and distracted, I shucked

the rest of my clothes and pressed my body to hers, skin to skin.

Her softness drove me wild.

Every curve, every jiggle, every little shiver when I dragged my teeth down her neck.

She was hot under me, flushed and panting.

"Damn, Darlin', you're fire," I murmured, brushing my nose against hers.

"No fever, huh?" she asked, teasing. "Just hot for me?"

"Exactly," I said, and nipped her lip.

She tasted like wine and strawberries and magic.

And every time she sighed, I caught glimpses of her thoughts, unfiltered and raw.

She wanted to be wanted. Needed to feel cherished.

Seen.

And I saw her.

Every glorious inch.

I worshipped her breasts, swirling my tongue around her nipples until she was squirming beneath me, hands in my hair, muttering spells between breathless moans.

She was thinking—*he's not mine, he can't be.*

But she wanted it. All of it.

"I am yours, Evie," I said, voice low and guttural. "Only yours."

Her gasp echoed through the room.

Then I took her.

With one hard thrust, I filled her, and she welcomed me like she was made for it.

My name on her lips, her legs wrapped around my waist.

She fit me perfectly, like we were carved from the same stone.

Her magic pulsed with mine, blue sparks flaring between us. It should've surprised me, but it didn't.

It felt right. Natural. Fated.

"Fuck," I groaned, buried to the hilt. "You feel so damn good."

She trembled beneath me, her lips parting in bliss as I started to move. Slowly at first, letting her adjust, then deeper, faster, harder. She met me thrust for thrust, hips rising to meet mine.

"Evie. My Darlin'," I murmured, kissing her as our rhythm quickened.

She was everything.

Soft, strong, sweet, wild.

She wore so many hats. Mayor. Witch. Friends. And all mattered to me, but this one?

This was just for us.

Mine. My mate.

I saw her try to fight it. Try to keep herself from falling—but she was already gone. Same as me. We were both falling fast.

Her inner voice whispered fears.

That she'd never be free to love.

That her duty to this town would always come first.

But she was wrong. And I was going to show her.

"Let me in," I growled, rolling my hips just right. "Let me be yours, my sweet Witch."

She moaned so loud I thought I'd come right then and there.

Her nails raked down my back, the magic inside her lighting up as she neared the edge.

We were fire and storm.

Moonlight and shadow.

Everything old and sacred in one perfect, tangled mess.

I reached between us and found her clit, rubbing in tight little circles, and that was all it took.

She came with a cry of my name, magic bursting from her fingertips in aqua sparks that zapped my ass like a Witchy love tap.

"Ouch," I chuckled, still grinding into her. "Sassy little thing."

But I didn't stop. Couldn't. I came with a roar, spilling inside her as my Wolf howled his claim.

The room glowed with something more than lamplight.

I wasn't sure if it was magic or fate, but I welcomed it.

I didn't move right away. Didn't want to leave her warmth.

But finally, I rolled to the side and pulled her with me, her soft curves molding to my body.

She was still catching her breath, mind racing with all the reasons this shouldn't work. Why other men had failed to keep her.

"There won't be any more *other men*, Darlin'," I muttered. "Otherwise, you're gonna have one hell of a killin' spree on your hands."

Her giggle was breathy and raw, but real.

"What are you saying?"

"I was right the first time," I said, kissing her temple. "You're my mate, Evelyn Castor."

Well, fuck me sideways, she thought.

I smirked. "Whatever you want, Darlin'."

And then I gave it to her—*sideways, and all the other ways, again and again*—until she forgot her name, forgot the town, forgot everything except the two of us tangled together, where we belonged.

Later, I fed her chocolate mousse and strawberries in bed.

Watched her try not to ask me to stay.

I kissed her and left anyway, because I wanted her to want me back for more than one night.

And I would be back.

That little Witch was mine now.

CHAPTER EIGHTEEN-EVIE

"SOMEONE IS AT YOUR DOOR. They've been knocking for ten minutes now, and I have a headache from your cheap vodka."

The voice was gravelly, nasal, and full of shade. I blinked awake to find Ivan standing on my night-stand, arms crossed over his hairy little chest, his fur puffed out like a pissed-off cat.

"OW!" he screeched when I zapped his butt with a flick of my fingers. A soft pulse of aqua-blue magic lit up the room as my Domovyk familiar flew off the furniture with an indignant yelp.

"That's abuse! I will be reporting this to the Morrigan!"

"Tell her to get in line," I mumbled, groaning as I

rolled over. "And you better make an appointment first."

I grinned as he stomped from the room, muttering curses in ancient Slavic, probably about my taste in booze.

He wasn't wrong about the vodka—*it had been cheap*—but what did he expect?

I was a small-town mayor with a supernatural community to wrangle and a very, very satisfying lover to recover from.

Speaking of that.

Mmm. Jaxson.

Even half-asleep, my body tingled with leftover magic and delicious soreness in all the right places. I'd been having the most amazing dream—something about Jaxson feeding me zabaglione while naked, the custard warm and creamy on his fingers as he—*what the?*

KNOCK KNOCK KNOCK KNOCK KNOCK!

"UGH. For Gaia's sake," I groaned, dragging myself upright and stumbling to the window.

I peeked through the blinds and immediately wanted to crawl back under the covers.

"Miss Spritely?" I called down.

The older Witch stood on my stoop, arms

crossed, mouth pursed into a wrinkled scowl that could curdle fresh milk.

"I'll be right there!" I called quickly and ducked back inside before she hexed me for tardiness.

With no time for proper grooming, I opted for my go-to cheat—*magic.*

Quick spell, flash of light, and poof! Showered, dressed, and reasonably deodorized.

Was it as satisfying as a long soak in my rosemary-lavender bath salts?

No.

But desperate times, etc.

I tugged on a soft peach dress, threw on a coordinating cardigan, and stepped into my sensible, one-inch nude heels—because fashionable mayor required some heel, but practical Witch refused to twist an ankle over aesthetics.

I caught my reflection in the hall mirror and gave myself a once-over. Not bad.

Hair wasn't frizzing.

Dress was cute.

I looked like a woman who'd definitely not spent the night getting thoroughly ravished by a silver-eyed Werewolf who made me come so hard I saw stars.

Twice.

Ivan glared at me from the arm of the couch as I passed through the living room.

"I hope you remember to file your paperwork for that magical shower. Regulations exist for a reason."

I waved him off with a tight-lipped smile. "Love you too, *grumpasaurus*."

He harrumphed and turned away, but not before I noticed the twigs and leaves, he'd decorated the dumbwaiter door with.

Why? No idea.

Was it weirdly charming? Kinda.

Would I let him keep doing it? Probably.

The little beast had clawed his way into my heart, even if he did leave the toilet seat up like a frat Goblin.

But then I passed the kitchen—and stopped dead.

"Oh no, absolutely not."

Chaos.

Dirty pans, crusty bowls, and a stack of unwashed plates that leaned at a dangerous angle like the damn Tower of Pisa.

"Ivan!" I called, spinning around.

He looked up innocently. Too innocently.

"Those aren't mine," I snapped. "Or Jaxson's."

He shrugged. "I had an early breakfast. And second breakfast. And a pre-lunch snack."

"You ate seven eggs yesterday, you hairy garbage disposal!"

"They were deviled, and you said I was your guest."

I resisted the urge to fry his tail again and kept moving.

The sexy high of post-coital bliss was slowly evaporating under the weight of dirty dishes and door-banging Witches.

But still, nothing could completely ruin my morning.

Not after a night like that.

Jaxson Reid had rocked my world.

Emotionally. Physically. Spiritually. Cosmically, even.

That man was sent by Gaia herself, and he knew exactly how to use his hands.

And his mouth.

And his—*I fanned my face.*

Focus, Evie.

I was not going to get sidetracked thinking about how he licked me like I was the last slice of peach pie at the Harvest Festival.

Or how he fed me chocolate mousse and zabaglione in bed like a gentleman, then made me scream like a heathen.

Nope. Not thinking about it.

Except, now I was wondering if he'd come back tonight.

For dessert. Or dinner. Or both.

In that order or reversed.

Goddess help me, I was sure the man could make a tuna melt taste like foreplay.

Just thinking about his lemon-basil scent had me clenching.

Was there a word for being totally, unapologetically, out-of-your-mind dick-whipped?

Cock-mused? Wolf-struck? Mate-ridden?

I needed to get a grip. I was the mayor. I had responsibilities.

A town full of Shifters, Witches, and wandering Fae.

I couldn't go swooning over every hard-bodied newcomer with a jawline sharp enough to cut glass and a cock that made me forget my own damn name.

Just one.

One cock.

One jawline.

One growly, possessive, maddeningly perfect Wolf.

And why not? My inner voice purred. *It's not like he didn't earn it.*

I couldn't even argue.

The only mistake I made last night was letting him leave.

Another knock rattled the whole damn house.

"HELLO! EVELYN CASTOR, OPEN THIS DOOR!"

I winced. Miss Spritely was not going to be pleased. Hopefully she was here about potholes and not the flare of blue sparks that exploded from my chimney around midnight.

"Coming!" I shouted, hustling to the door.

Still flushed from my memories.

Still grinning like a teenager.

Still hoping Jaxson showed up again tonight.

And maybe the night after that.

Because, ready or not, I had a feeling my Wolf wasn't done with me.

And I wasn't even close to being done with him.

Thoughts of bedrooms and sexy Wolves fled my brain at the sound of my old principal's harsh voice.

Guess it was back to work for me.

Saturdays be damned.

Ugh.

Miss Spritely banged on the door again, along with her accompanying yell. I closed my eyes, praying to Gaia for patience.

Ivan growled his annoyance.

The Domovyk then scurried away to his dumb-waiter/hideout/nest.

Looked like I was on my own for this one. I didn't know much about having a familiar, but Ivan and I would muddle through it.

Not like I had much choice since the almighty *Witch Wheedler*, aka La Befana, sent the little creatures to me and my besties.

"One moment!" I shouted and opened the door. "Miss Spritely, how nice to see you this morning."

Did I say that? Well, I lied.

The pinched face of the school principal greeted me, and I backed up a step.

My most polite mayor's smile did nothing to soften her harsh stare, and I stepped aside to avoid being trampled.

"This is unacceptable, Evelyn. I warned you something was going on and now we have two students missing!" Miss Spritely hissed and handed me a hot off the presses copy of *The Daily Corner*.

How did the town's only paper do it?

The Corner, as it was nicknamed, was somehow created with one journalist/editor, a decidedly unpopular Wizard named Iggy Barrens.

The pinch-faced man always seemed to be one step ahead with the local gossip and news.

It was beyond me!

Must be magic, but I swear I detected nothing extraordinary when I ran into the little creep.

Wizards, in general, were not very savory.

That he was a journalist made it even worse.

"Did you call the sheriff?" I asked.

"Sheriff Davis is a one-hundred-and-seventy-year-old goat Shifter, Madam Mayor. What exactly is he going to do?"

"His job?" I said, though it came out sounding more like a question.

"No! Evie, it is up to you. As our mayor and the last remaining Castor, you must investigate. How could this happen? And letting in those Shifters too? No. No. it is your duty as a Castor to make this right."

With that final word, Miss Spritely stormed out of my house.

Leaving me feeling exactly the same as I had back in sixth grade when I'd failed to turn in my homework two nights in a row because I'd binge-read the entire *Sweet Valley High* book series by Francine Pascal.

Before I could work myself up into a frenzy, my

laptop started trilling, and I recognized the sound as a Swoosh call coming in.

What the freak now?

Seriously. If it wasn't one thing, it was something else!

Now, who might this be?

I blew out an exasperated breath and stalked over to the small corner desk I'd put in the living room by the back window overlooking my yard.

I liked natural light when I was working.

Now that it was fall, the leaves were turning beautiful shades of gold and red. I enjoyed the view very much.

The barrage of interruptions this Saturday morning—*meh, not so much.*

"EVELYN CASTOR, BY THE GODDESS' PERFECTLY PROPORTIONED ASSETS, YOU BETTER COME GET THIS LITTLE SHIT OUT OF MY HOUSE RIGHT NOW!"

Donny's voice hit my ears like a banshee with a megaphone. It roared through the two tiny, enchanted speakers perched beside my laptop, which rattled ominously under the audio onslaught.

"Evie! I swear to Gaia, this little hairy demon is testing me!"

It took a second for the visual to catch up—

Swoosh always lagged a bit when it was heavy on the rage-fueled spellcasting.

Swoosh, for the record, was the Witch community's magic-based answer to Zoom.

You couldn't exactly trust traditional cell service when your blood ran hexes and high-voltage vibes.

Witch magic and electricity didn't mix well.

Think Mentos and Diet Coke with sparks.

I blinked at the purple mist swirling inside my screen as the image loaded.

"One sec, Donny, I can't see what's going on."

"Oh, I'll tell you what's going on!" she screeched, like a banshee who moonlit as a New Jersey hairdresser.

"This Domo-dick is LEAVING SURPRISES."

And just like that, the mist cleared and the full wrath of Donatella the Destroyer was upon me.

Hair frizzed, cheeks flushed, and eyes glittering with murder.

She angled her phone's crystal-ball lens and—ugh.

I instantly regretted it.

The floor of her salon looked like a unicorn had gotten violently ill after eating too many flaming Cheetos and jellybeans.

Glowing piles of neon orange and slime-green poop littered the sleek black tile.

One particularly menacing turd sat nestled inside a leopard-print stiletto like it paid rent there.

I slapped a hand over my eyes.

"Oh, gross! Donny!"

"GROSS?!" she shrieked. "GROSS is hardly adequate for fishing this Day-Glo demon dung out of my favorite pair of Louboutins!"

"I didn't even know you owned Louboutins," I mumbled.

"They were secondhand! BUT THEY WERE STILL MINE."

She kicked the shoe across the room, narrowly missing her freshly enchanted shampoo station.

The thud it made echoed with finality.

"Okay, deep breaths," I offered, ever the sensible one. "You just need to talk to your familiar and maybe establish some basic boundaries—"

"BOUNDARIES? Evie, this thing pooped in my incense burner and spelled it to smell like burned licorice and Ogre ass hairs! Boundaries left the chat the moment this Domo-bastard decided to go ape shit-literally!"

Suddenly, her eyes darted to the side.

"There you are, you hairy little turd dropper!"

I saw the blur before the crash.

Donatella dove across the screen like an NFL linebacker, aiming straight for the broom closet.

If the New York Giants hired her, their record might actually improve.

But the thought was gone the second her phone hit the floor.

Now, the camera was filming sideways chaos as couch cushions flew through the air and a furious string of curses filled the audio feed.

"I'm gonna bleach your entire body! I'll wax a stripe down your fuzzy ass like a racing skunk! You'll be the first Domovyk to be neutered by salon shears!"

"Yikes," I whispered, wincing as something shattered offscreen.

A small puff of orange fur flew past the screen.

I stared for a second, then calmly reached for my Swoosh dial.

"Maribella, you better get over there before Donny commits supernatural war crimes."

To her credit, Bella picked up right away.

Her image shimmered into place with a bright, cheery glow and a halo of sunshine framing her perfectly curled golden locks.

She looked like a walking Pinterest board.

Figures.

"Evie! Why are you shouting? I could hear you all the way from—oh." She tilted her head, noting my expression. "Let me guess, Donny again?"

I sighed. "She's on a rampage. Her Domovyk—Grady? Grover?"

"Gryn," she corrected with a patient smile. "Honestly, Evie, it's four letters."

"Right, Gryn. He's redecorating her life in poop emojis—neon green ones—and Donatella is threatening to Nair him bald. I figured I'd call you before she ends up with a Domovyk pelt rug."

Bella snorted. "Okay, okay, I'll go talk her down. Petyr and I were just having some tea anyway. He was telling me the funniest story about a squirrel who got turned into a bar of soap—"

"Sounds delightful," I cut in. "But we've got bigger issues. Two kids aren't accounted for over by the cemetery."

Bella sobered instantly. "What? Evie, that's sheriff territory."

I gave a one-shoulder shrug.

"Apparently not anymore. The vibes are spooky, and the Sheriff said it's Trifecta business now."

She muttered something that sounded suspiciously like *useless Weregoat*, but nodded.

"Alright. I'll check on Donny. But for the record, you all need to start treating these Domovyks like the sweet, sentient beings they are. They're sensitive, powerful, and practically immortal."

"Uh-huh," I said. "Tell that to the pile of nuclear feces that just tried to assimilate Donny's decorative throw pillows."

"And you could be nicer to your Domovyk," she said with a pointed arch of her brows. "Ivan's been doing his best."

"Ivan electrocuted my houseplants and left fur in the refrigerator," I reminded her. "And I'm almost sure he stole my vibrator to use as a back massager."

"Boundaries, Evie," Bella said sweetly, giggling at something Petyr said and winking at him saucily.

Boundaries, huh?

We shall see.

I sighed and gripped the lid on my laptop.

Between glowing poop, Witch-on-Domovyk warfare, and magical Swoosh calls with a laggy spell buffer, it was just another day in Castor's Corner.

Now I had a haunted cemetery and two missing kids to check on.

At least I had my sensible shoes on.

And, *if Gaia loved me at all,* maybe a smexy Wolf waiting for me tonight with dessert in bed and a firm hand on my ass.

A Witch could hope.

CHAPTER NINETEEN-EVIE

"BY THE WAY, UM," Maribella's voice slowed, a classic sign she was about to veer from pastries into personal drama.

Her heart-shaped face in the Swoosh screen looked unusually uncertain, eyes flicking toward her shoulder like she was checking for eavesdropping familiars.

"How long are those Shifters staying?"

I exhaled slowly and leaned back in my chair, stretching out the kinks in my neck.

"I don't know," I said, as honestly as I could.

And that was the problem, wasn't it? I didn't know.

Jaxson hadn't said anything definite, and I'd been too busy fantasizing about him spoon-feeding me chocolate mousse and zabaglione in bed to bring it up.

Pathetic, right? I know.

I wanted him to stay.

I wanted the time to explore whatever this thing was between us.

Something hot and magical and, dare I say, meaningful.

But was wanting enough?

Could I risk the balance of Castor's Corner for the sake of a whirlwind romance and some truly orgasmic kissing?

Yeah, probably not.

Sometimes being the responsible adult really sucked magical goat balls.

And there was the annoying fact that even though he saw my O face mondo times last night, Jaxson didn't claim me.

He didn't mark me with his bite.

And I was like ninety-nine point nine percent sure that was how it was done.

"Maybe the kids just ran off to the woods to play hooky from Miss Spritely's evil Saturday morning lessons?" Maribella suggested, trying to lift my suddenly dour mood.

"Could be," I said. "Or they stumbled into another

realm and are now apprenticing with a squirrel Wizard. Honestly, it's a toss-up."

"Evie?" she said gently, drawing me back from my sarcasm spiral.

"What?"

Her face softened even more. She bit her lower lip—classic Maribella when she was about to ask something big.

Then she said, "Do you think, um, do you think we could keep them?"

I blinked. "Keep who?"

But I already knew.

The second the words left my mouth, my stomach did a somersault.

My gaze drifted to the dancing donuts she'd enchanted around her Swoosh frame.

I'd gotten used to their frosting-fueled frolicking, but at that moment, they seemed unusually smug.

Like they knew something I didn't.

Maribella gave me that look—*the one that meant you know exactly who I'm talking about, Evie Castor, don't play dumb.*

"Has something happened between you and one of the guys?" I asked, narrowing my eyes.

"Of course not," she said instantly.

Too instantly.

And then came the sniff.

Not a sad sniff.

No, a guilty one.

The Maribella Special.

She sniffed like that every time she *accidentally* let a customer have a free cookie or told someone their baby was cute when it actually looked like a potato.

"Mm hmm," I said, crossing my arms.

Her cheeks turned the color of strawberry buttercream.

"I said of course not!" she repeated, and then added in a much smaller voice, "But maybe there's, um, potential."

I arched a brow. "Uh huh. Potential. That's what we're calling it now?"

She huffed, then glanced over her shoulder like the walls might be listening.

"It will keep," she muttered. "Now you be careful, Evie."

Her expression changed so fast it gave me whiplash.

Gone was the flustered bakery flirt.

In her place was Witch Oracle Mode, eyes soft and steady.

I didn't take it lightly.

Sure, I was the one with the official Sight, but

Maribella had instincts that could rival a bloodhound.

And when she looked at me like that, I knew something was stirring.

"Do you think I should come with you?" she asked quietly.

"Nonsense," I said, brushing her off with a wave. "You've got a bakery to run. And a zero-carb brownie recipe to perfect. I believe in you."

She groaned. "Right. So much for our legendary Witch metabolism."

"Well, Italian Witches are different, Bella. You know how it works. My ancestors descended from the OG La Befana," I said, quoting Nonna's favorite lore.

"Pasta first, magic second."

"Yeah, well, I'm only Italian by association. Any actual Italian blood is so far back in my gene pool it hardly counts," she grumbled. "So shouldn't I only gain like a portion of the weight?"

"That's not how carbs work. If it were, I'd have a full six-pack instead of a marshmallow center and thighs that jiggle when I sneeze."

We shared a laugh, and something in my chest unclenched.

No matter what was coming, I had these two incredible Witches at my back.

And that meant the world.

Maribella sighed again, softer this time. "I'll work on the brownies if you promise to be careful."

I held up three fingers in the most solemn vow we had. "Witch's honor."

She rolled her eyes. "Fine. But call if you need me. I mean it, Evie. If anything feels off—*anything at all*—you call me and I'll be there. Petyr can hold down the bakery for a few hours."

"I will," I said, meaning it. "Now go wrestle with your feelings for whichever sexy Shifter you're not dating but might maybe want to do naked kitchen magic with."

She turned as red as her raspberry glaze and ended the call with a sputter and a snap.

I smiled as the donuts winked out and the screen went dark.

Despite the swirling magic, the missing kids, and the Shifters camping out in my sleepy little town, I was smiling.

Gods help me.

Because the real trouble hadn't even started yet.

We signed off at the same time, but I stayed put, just breathing, fingers still curled around my teacup like it might anchor me to the calm before the chaos.

My eyes drifted to the Swoosh screen, now dark, and then to the soft hum of the town beyond my window.

Guilt-free brownies.

Goddess bless Maribella and her endless baking optimism.

It was practically the Holy Grail of our friendship—three curvy Witches on a lifelong quest to enjoy dessert without it going straight to our asses, boobs, or bellies.

So far, the quest had yielded *very* delicious failures, several sugar comas, and exactly one singed oven mitt from Donatella trying to *infuse* her brownies with a fire rune.

Witch metabolism, my ass.

No, seriously.

My *actual* ass.

The one that I had inherited from my Great Aunt Edna.

The one that made its presence known in every pair of leggings I owned.

Somewhere in the great cosmic blueprint, the magical beings upstairs had decided the Trifecta would wield immense power, run an entire supernatural town, and have hips that didn't lie—but did jiggle.

A whole fucking lot.

Maribella used to say it was the *Jersey Girl* in us.

Nonna said it was the Benevento blood of my ancestors. Witches from southern Italy had a love affair with carbs and spells passed down by Nonna, and both had consequences.

Mainly, the kind that settled in the lower half and refused to budge.

Pasta was in my bones.

Cannoli in my destiny.

And don't even get me started on tiramisu.

That stuff was basically a love potion.

I sighed and glanced down at myself. Sure, I had a few extra curves.

And yeah, sometimes it stung when I stood next to twigs like the Great Witch Wheedler, who still looked like a walking enchantment even after birthing twins.

But last night?

Last night, Jaxson had devoured every inch of me like I was a Michelin-star meal, dessert, and a double shot of whiskey all rolled into one.

And not once did he hesitate.

Not once did he flinch or falter.

If anything, he looked at me like he *thanked* the stars I wasn't built differently.

Or like a stick.

That kind of appreciation?

It wasn't just sex.

It was like being worshipped and I was so down for more.

A slow, smug smile crept across my face.

I wasn't that chubby sixteen-year-old anymore.

The one who could barely control her magic or her hormones.

Who'd crushed on the quarterback and flamed her eyebrows off trying to cast a glamour charm.

I was a grown-ass woman.

A Witch. A protector. And, apparently, a sex goddess if last night's performance review counted.

Yowza, indeed.

My phone buzzed on the desk, snapping me out of my little victory montage. I peeked at the screen— Donatella.

Of course.

She warned me to stay alert and offered to come with. I could practically hear her voice in the message, crisp with concern and thinly veiled anxiety.

Maribella must've tipped her off about the cemetery errand.

I texted back quickly.

ME

Got this. All good. Go clean up your demon poop.

She replied with a skull emoji and what I *think* was a GIF of a Wiccan smudging a bathroom.

I exhaled, stood up, and rolled my shoulders.

Time to shake off the dreamy afterglow and get back in mayor mode.

Two kids were missing.

That wasn't just a blip on my to-do list—it was a full-blown,   red-alert,   boots-on-the-ground situation.

Whoever thought they could mess with innocents in *my* town was in for a rude awakening.

Castor's Corner wasn't just my home.

It was my responsibility.

And when it came to right and wrong, I didn't screw around.

Harming children?

That was the kind of evil that made my blood simmer.

I reached inward, checking my magical reserves.

Yep. Still buzzing like a live wire.

Turns out, orgasms were nature's power boost.

Maybe I should add it to the next town council wellness memo.

For best results, channel sexual energy responsibly. May cause spontaneous magical surges and enhanced glow.

Still, as much as I hated to admit it, a pang shot through my chest when I thought of Jaxson leaving.

Which he probably would.

Probably *should.*

His Pack, his mission—*hell, his entire life*—wasn't rooted here.

But I was.

And yet, I had to wonder.

The way he'd looked at me last night? Like he'd been searching for something his whole damn life and just found it tangled up in my sheets?

Yeah. That look haunted me in the best possible way.

Was I being selfish, wanting to keep him here?

Absolutely.

Would I do it anyway if I thought it wouldn't hurt anyone else?

You bet your sweet, carb-loving, Italian Witch ass I would.

I shook it off.

Later.

I could moon over Werewolves after I ensured the town's kids were safe and sound.

I cracked my knuckles and stretched my arms overhead, letting the tension snap loose from my spine.

No more stalling.

I had magic.

I had motive.

I had murderously maternal instincts.

And if whoever took those kids didn't want to deal with the full wrath of a sexually recharged Witch with a caffeine addiction and a wicked right hook—*they'd best return them now.*

I was about to go full Hex Mode.

Big girl panties: on.

Mission: active.

Ass-kicking: imminent.

Because nobody—and I mean *nobody*—messed with my town.

Not on my watch.

CHAPTER TWENTY-JAXSON

WAITING for the sun to set was pure torture.

I'd paced the damn room so many times I was starting to wear a path in the floorboards.

It wasn't just the anticipation that had me keyed up.

It was *her*. Evie Castor.

Curvy, brilliant, stubborn as hell. And all mine. I could still taste her on my tongue.

Still feel her nails in my back.

Still hear the soft way she whispered my name when she thought I was asleep.

Damn. That woman was gonna be the death of me— and I'd die smiling.

"Oh my Goddess," Ryan groaned from his bed. "Do you *mind*, Jax? Some of us aren't getting any and don't appreciate the love-sick Wolf pacing the floor like he's starring in a bad country song."

I looked over.

The big Grizzly was sprawled on his back, an arm over his eyes, radiating all kinds of sulky energy.

"What's the matter, Ry? You allergic to joy?"

"I'm allergic to the *scent* of joy," he snapped. "You smell like sex and pesto, and it's making me homicidal."

"Well, that's not very community-minded of you," I said, grabbing a pillow off the couch and lobbing it at his head.

"Just because your Witch hasn't noticed you yet doesn't mean you have to rain on my afterglow."

"She *growled* at me, Jaxson. Growled. Like I was interrupting her snack time or something."

"She probably *was* snacking," Conrad muttered from the kitchen table, where he was currently doodling something that looked suspiciously like a heart with initials in it. "Bella likes snacking, too."

Ryan sat up and pointed at him. "See? You get it. We're two grown-ass Shifters stuck in romantic limbo while *Romeo* over there is already halfway to moving in and naming their future pups."

I couldn't help but grin.

"You jealous bastards will get your shot. Just gotta be patient."

"Easy for you to say," Ryan grumbled. "Your girl licked whipped cream off your chest, and you haven't stopped smiling since."

"She did more than that. She scratched me," I corrected proudly. "Right here." I tapped my shoulder. "It was hot."

Conrad actually sighed.

"I think my Dad said scratching and biting is a good sign in magical-mate culture. Maybe it means the bond is strengthening?"

Ryan rolled his eyes. "You and your bedtime stories. Goddess help us all."

I leaned against the wall and crossed my arms. "Look, if we're serious about staying—*and I mean really staying*—we need to do more than smile at the locals and raid Bella's bakery and the local diner for meals."

"We pay for all our muffins!" Ryan said indignantly.

"Yeah, but she keeps giving us freebies, sweet, soft-hearted Witch," Conrad pointed out. "Which I'm not mad about. But Jax has a point. We need jobs. Roots. *Purpose*."

"Exactly," I said. "And speaking of purpose," I say

and let the sentence trail off as I pulled a piece of paper from my back pocket and waved it around.

"What's that?" Ryan asked suspiciously.

"An idea," I grinned. "Or rather, an opportunity. Our neighbor, Councilwoman Levy—you know, the silver-haired Tigress who keeps pretending to garden just so she can eavesdrop on our conversations?"

"She complimented my ass last night before I turned in," Conrad said.

"She pinched mine," Ryan muttered. "I'm still emotionally recovering."

"Well, gird your loins, boys, because she wants us for the *fire department*."

There was a beat of stunned silence.

"She *what*?" Ryan asked.

"She said Castor's Corner could use a few strapping young men with muscles and rescue instincts. Apparently, the old crew's half-retired, and we look like the kind of men who can hold a hose."

Conrad blinked. "Did she actually say that? About the hose?"

"She said, and I quote: *'I bet you boys know how to handle your equipment. We could use men like you at the station.'*"

Ryan snorted. "Did she wink when she said it?"

"Twice," I said. "One eye, then the other. Very coordinated."

Conrad leaned back in his chair, arms folded.

"So you're suggesting we become Castor's Corner's newest firefighters?"

"I'm suggesting we stop looking like a traveling supernatural boy band and start acting like part of the community. We want our women to take us seriously, right?"

Ryan scratched his chin. "I mean, you've got a point. Saving lives. Running into burning buildings. Wearing suspenders. Hats, even."

"Yeah, no shirt required. The ladies would love it," Conrad added dreamily.

"Alright, *Magic Mike*, cool it." I chuckled. "I'm just saying—it's more than a job. It's a message. We're not just passing through. We want to *build* something here. Protect this town. Help the people they care about."

"And," Conrad said, suddenly serious, "show them we're worthy."

We all nodded.

It wasn't about proving ourselves with muscles or charm or even sex appeal—though, let's be honest, we weren't lacking in that department.

It was about *intention*. About showing our mates that we weren't just after a fling.

We were after forever.

"Let's talk to Councilwoman Levy right now," I said, firming my voice and standing straight like this was a damn mission briefing.

"We'll set up a formal meeting later. Maybe get a tour of the firehouse. We show up, offer to train, volunteer—*whatever it takes*. No more waiting around like lost puppies."

Ryan let out a theatrical groan and flopped back onto the couch.

"Fine. But if she pinches me again, I swear I'm transferring to animal control. I'm not built for cougars, even if she *is* a literal Tiger."

"You're just mad she said you looked like a fuzzy sweet potato," Conrad quipped from the armchair, grinning like a loon.

"She said *snackable*, thank you very much," Ryan retorted. "Then, she winked, wheezed, and snorted. Simultaneously. That's not normal."

Conrad wiggled his brows.

"Deal. But dibs on the calendar shoot. I call October. I've already got a concept—*me, a hose, maybe some magical steam for effect—*"

"You *would* pick October, you basic bitch," Ryan said. "You just want to be the Halloween month."

"It's called branding," Conrad replied smugly.

I shook my head, chuckling under my breath as I grabbed my jacket.

"Come on, you clowns. Let's do this before one of you ends up hexed for public indecency. If we're going to make Castor's Corner home, we've got to *act* like it. No more loafing. It's time we earned the right to stay."

"Earn it, huh?" Ryan muttered, rising to his feet with a reluctant stretch.

"Guess there are worse things than being a hot firefighter in a town full of supernaturals when we got Witches to impress."

"Exactly," I said. "This isn't about the uniforms. It's about showing our mates we're not just passing through. We're here to protect what they love. To be part of it."

"Man, when you get like this, it's hard not to follow you," Conrad said, slapping my back as we made our way out the front door. "Your Wolf's got serious alpha vibes."

I shrugged. "I just know what I want. And I want to build something here—with her. With all of us."

We walked the few blocks to Councilwoman

Levy's house, a charming bungalow nestled beneath two enormous magnolia trees. Flower beds exploded in color along the walkway, and a row of wind chimes tinkled in the breeze, casting a faint hum of protective magic in the air. Classic Tigress.

I knocked three times.

The door swung open so fast I swear she'd been waiting behind it.

"Well, *dears*," Councilwoman Levy said, beaming like we were her favorite soap opera finally getting to the good part. "I was wondering when you'd get around to it."

I blinked. "How do you mean?"

She leaned against the doorframe, a feline smile spreading across her face.

"You three came here for a reason. You think fate plopped you into Castor's Corner by accident? Please. You've got that 'mate-tingle' all over you. And I haven't seen men with thighs like that since the last centaur parade."

Ryan made a strangled sound, but she wasn't done.

"Now," she continued, eyes twinkling, "let's see how you'll look in uniform."

She waggled her perfectly striped black-and-white eyebrows at us like some kind of magical fashion judge, then turned on her heel and strode back inside with the command of a queen.

We glanced at one another.

"She's terrifying," Ryan whispered.

"She's outrageous," Conrad murmured.

"She's our best shot," I said, grinning as we followed her in.

Because I wasn't leaving.

Not unless Evie told me to.

And even then, she'd have to cast a damn binding spell and hit me with a broom to make me go.

This wasn't a pit stop.

Castor's Corner was home now.

And I'd burn down every obstacle in my way to keep it.

CHAPTER TWENTY-ONE-EVIE

"GOOD MORNING," Stanley called out like we were about to brunch instead of confront whatever dark force was creeping around the Castor family cemetery.

He was leaning against his shiny hybrid like some kind of Pinterest apocalypse model—camouflage pants, a sheer mesh khaki long-sleeved shirt that showed off his surprisingly toned frame, and a pair of oversized sunglasses perched on his slicked-back hair.

"What are you doing here?" I asked, genuinely baffled and maybe a little suspicious he'd glamoured himself out of an editorial shoot.

"I'm your assistant," he said dryly, like I'd just asked him what two plus two was.

"Yes, but it's Saturday," I replied.

He blinked. "And?"

"And you don't work on Saturdays."

He scoffed and opened the car door for me with a dramatic flourish.

"A certain buxom blonde might have casually mentioned you were headed into the dead zone to investigate two missing children, so I figured—*just a thought here*—that maybe your assistant should assist?"

He shut the door after I got in, jogged around the hood of the car with the energy of someone who maybe did cardio twice a year, and collapsed into the driver's seat, breathing like he'd run a marathon.

I stared at him. "Stanley, are you winded?"

"No!" he panted. "I'm dramatically overwhelmed by the burden of your poor organizational choices."

Still, I was touched.

It wasn't often someone volunteered to follow me into creepy magical danger, let alone someone in mesh.

"Where to, boss?" he asked, peeling away from the curb like we were in a buddy cop movie.

"The cemetery," I said, trying to channel my inner badass despite the peach dress I was still wearing—

the same one I'd thrown on for Miss Spritely's door-pounding extravaganza.

Stanley pulled up to the cemetery gates, and I hopped out before he could launch into some monologue about ghost chic or graveyard fashion.

I took three steps, froze, and looked down at myself.

"Drat."

"Problem?" Stanley called from the car, adjusting his sunglasses like this was a photoshoot for 'Supernatural CEO Weekly.'

"I'm about to trudge through ancient mausoleums and god knows what else in a floaty dress and pumps. Gaia help me."

There was only one solution. I closed my eyes and whispered a quick spell:

"Gaia on high,
Grant my ask,
Change my outfit,
To prepare for this task,
A Witchy mayor
Is all that I am,
Your grace be with me,
And the children of Castor,
Be with us again."

The sky flashed.

Thunder cracked.

Purple and blue lightning spiraled overhead like a disco party hosted by the Divine.

I looked down. Still peach dress. Still heels.

"Rude," I muttered. "Was it the rhyming? Was that not up to par?"

"You look radiant," Stanley said. "Like a sacrificial virgin in a high-budget horror movie."

"Thanks," I deadpanned. "That's exactly the vibe I was going for."

"You ready?" he asked, reaching into the glove box for what I assumed was something useful.

"Stanley, that's a lint roller."

"A tactical lint roller," he corrected.

I sighed. "Look, I need you to stay here."

"But—Evie—"

"No buts. If something goes wrong, I need someone to call in the cavalry. Or at least the Coven."

He opened his mouth to argue again just as someone else shouted my name.

"Evelyn!"

I turned, and my ovaries did a backflip.

Jaxson.

Tight jeans.

Black T-shirt.

Biceps that could carry me—and they did last night.

One look at the big sexy Wolf and all my emotional baggage seemed to dissipate.

And behind him? Ryan and Conrad—looking like a bunch of magical henchmen no one asked for, but everyone wanted.

Ryan had grown a beard that was giving me 'Mountain Daddy' vibes, and Conrad was dressed in all white like he was about to summon an out of planet experience or host a very exclusive rave.

"Maribella told us what was going on," Jaxson said. "And we want to help."

Of course, she did.

Then, as if the universe had just unlocked a new level of chaos, I heard them.

"Evie!"

I turned again to see Maribella pedaling her bakery bike like the Wicked Witch of South Jersey—with Donny, in full glam and heels, perched on the handlebars like it was a runway challenge.

"Are you out of your damn minds?" I shouted.

"Don't you dare try this without us," Donny snapped, hopping down and wobbling slightly before regaining her footing like a warrior queen in Louboutins.

"You wore killer heels to the cemetery?" I asked.

She adjusted her leather trench coat. "I'm wearing enchanted insoles. Witch, please."

"Look," I started, raising my hands. "I appreciate the concern. Really. But I am the mayor. I have to go in there. It's my responsibility—"

"You're not doing it alone," Maribella said, climbing off her bike with the grace of someone who regularly jumps curbs with cupcakes.

"This is our town," Donny added. "We're the Trifecta. You go, we go."

Jaxson crossed his arms and gave me a look that said *you're stuck with me, sugar.*

"And I'm not letting you walk into danger without backup. You're my—"

He paused.

"You're important to me."

"Besides," Conrad said, holding up a wand made of what suspiciously looked like a baguette. "We brought snacks."

"And protection." Ryan unleashed his claws.

I blinked at them all.

My heart felt like a carousel of chaos and love and possibly carbs.

"Fine," I huffed. "But if anything comes flying at us, Donny's on decapitation duty."

Donny cracked her knuckles. "Finally. Something fun."

"Maribella, you're the shield. Stanley—"

"I'll handle logistics and document the moment for posterity," he said, already pulling out his phone.

"And Jaxson." I met his gaze. "You're with me."

He smirked.

"Always."

Together, we stepped toward the iron gates, my peach dress flapping in the breeze like a flag of slightly unhinged courage.

My motley crew behind me, the weirdest support system a Witch could ask for.

Let the creepy cemetery showdown begin.

CHAPTER TWENTY-TWO-EVIE

"UM, BEFORE WE GO IN THERE," I said, turning to face the group gathering behind me, "I just want to say—if this starts looking dicey, all of you need to go. No arguments."

There was a beat of silence.

"Not happening," Jaxson said immediately, his tone like iron wrapped in velvet.

I turned to him, heart thudding. "Jaxson, you're not even from here. You don't have to risk anything for this town. For me."

He stepped forward, closing the space between us like it was nothing.

"That's where you're wrong, Darlin'. You are *exactly* why I'm here. And this town? It's your heart. That makes it mine, too."

My throat worked around a knot I couldn't quite swallow.

Gaia help me, I wanted to kiss him again. But now wasn't the time.

Not with the sky turning a sickly green, grayish color just over the cemetery gates and a thick wave of dread rolling off the place like fog from the River Styx.

Ryan gave a dramatic sigh. "We're not leaving either."

Conrad nodded. "We might not have magic, but we've got claws and muscle and really great hair. We're in."

Donny crossed her arms, still seated sidesaddle on Maribella's handlebars. "You *know* we're not going anywhere. I already canceled my blowout appointment for this."

"Which was very brave of her," Maribella chimed in, breathless from pedaling uphill in wedge heels.

I gave a shaky laugh and looked at the people surrounding me—this ridiculous, brave, wonderful mess of a group—and my heart squeezed.

They weren't just backing me.

They *believed* in me.

And that was something I hadn't felt in a long, long time.

"But if it makes you feel better," Jaxson said, then turned. "Where is your sheriff?" he asked, voice steady but tight with concern.

As if summoned by name—and probably overhearing everything with those ridiculous goat ears—Sheriff Davis slowly made his way up Main Street.

Stooped and wiry, the ancient goat Shifter moved like molasses on a cold day.

His tweed jacket flapped in the breeze like a cape, though the only thing he'd battled lately was high cholesterol.

"Someone say my name?" he wheezed when he finally reached us.

Honestly, I loved the old coot. But he couldn't even outpace Miss Spritely on market day, let alone fight off the creeping darkness that was currently twisting its way over my family's cemetery gates like a demonic kudzu vine.

I turned just in time to see the iron bars pulse with oily green ooze, the sky above them darkening to the kind of gray that screamed *bad omens ahead*.

"No disrespect, Sheriff," Jaxson said, jaw tight, "but Evelyn is about to go in there alone to find two kids who vanished on their way to lessons this morning. Don't you think that's your job?"

The old goat Shifter gave Jaxson a long look before shaking his head slowly.

"Son, I've had a good long run, but I wouldn't last five minutes in a tussle with whatever's behind that gate."

I opened my mouth to speak, heart pounding.

I didn't want Jaxson to get more involved than he already was.

But before I could say anything—he opened his big, dumb, Wolfy mouth.

"Deputize me," Jaxson said, turning to the sheriff.

"You can't—" I began, stepping toward him.

He looked at me then—*really looked*—and my words froze in my throat.

"I respect you, Evelyn. And I know you've got more magic in your pinky than I do in my whole body. But you are *not* going in there alone." His voice was calm, firm. "Deputize me."

Sheriff Davis let out a low grunt and nodded. "I'll do you one better."

With a few ancient words that shimmered with quiet power, the goat Shifter removed the badge from his chest and pressed it into Jaxson's palm.

My eyes went wide. "What have you done?"

Jaxson didn't hesitate. "Whatever I can to protect you."

My throat closed. I'd faced Vampires, Banshees, and a Slime Demon with halitosis so bad it melted fences—but this?

This was terrifying.

Because it was love.

Or the beginning of it.

"I know it's fast for you," he continued, his silver-gray eyes locking with mine, "but we Shifters *know* when we've found our mates, Evie. I'll do anything to give you the time you need to accept it. But I can't do that if you go off and get yourself killed. So, now that I'm the interim sheriff of Castor's Corner—at least until a proper election can be held—I'm going in there with you, Madam Mayor."

My chest cracked open like a spell jar dropped from the top shelf.

No man had ever put himself on the line for me like this. Not once.

My whole life had been a series of me getting shit *done* because no one else would.

I was the responsible one, the strong one, the Witch who kept the lid on the town and the smile on her face.

And here was this man—this *Wolf*—trying to share the weight.

Trying to keep me safe.

My heart thundered as I crossed the distance between us. I reached for him, fisting my hands in his shirt, pulling him down, and kissed him. Slow. Deep. With every ounce of the impossible storm of affection and gratitude and lust I felt tangled up inside me.

When I pulled back, his eyes were a little glassy. Then, the confusion hit.

"Forgive me," I whispered.

His brows pulled together. "Evie—?"

And that's when the paralysis spell hit him.

Mid-sentence.

Jaxson's muscles locked up, and his body froze just as he realized what I'd done.

"Hold him up!" I barked to Ryan and Conrad.

Thank Gaia for Shifter reflexes.

They caught him before he went full tree trunk and smacked the pavement.

I turned toward the growing crowd, my voice strong even as my heart fractured.

"No one is to follow me. Not even him. The spell will wear off in an hour. I *will* be back by then."

"Evie—" Donny started.

"I have to," I said simply. "If something happens to me, it's on you two to keep the town safe. You know that."

Maribella looked stricken, but she nodded.

Every Witch has a crucible.

A reckoning.

This was mine.

I felt the power hum inside me.

Stronger than before.

Full and rich and ready to burn down whatever lay beyond those gates.

Not because I was reckless.

Because I was *ready*.

I straightened my spine, lifted my chin, and stepped toward the gate.

The vines peeled back like they *knew* I was coming.

"Well, that was spooky as fuck," Maribella whispered, barely audible.

"Shh," I said.

"Sorry."

With one last glance at my friends—*my sisters*—and the man who would walk through fire for me, I crossed the threshold.

This was my moment.

And I wasn't afraid anymore.

CHAPTER TWENTY-THREE-
EVIE

THE PATH WAS COVERED in that same glowing green ooze, and I swear it was bubbling.

Gross.

A ghastly howl filtered through the branches of the seasonably multicolored trees and shrubs that dotted the cemetery landscape, like fall had joined a horror movie shoot without getting a script.

And still I pressed forward, because I knew exactly where I was going.

I was angry. Confused. And okay—maybe a little queasy.

But mostly mad. Because this?

This could not be happening.

A Castor—*my family*—behind this supernatural slime-fest?

No freaking way.

We were the caretakers of this town. We ran the damn place.

Five minutes later, I was standing in front of the Castorini mausoleum.

The ancient stone bore the original name of my family—*before the Castorini-to-Castor rebrand had taken place somewhere between Ellis Island and the great American assimilation circus.*

The air was thick with rot and nostalgia.

Generations of my people were laid to rest behind those marble doors.

One day, I was supposed to join them.

Cue dramatic shudder.

Yeah, not today, Satan. Or slime. Or whatever this was.

My eyes flicked over the plaque that read Alfonso Castor—*my grandfather*—and yep, just as I feared, that nasty, glowing, minty slime was now oozing out of the engraving and forming trails that reached out like evil fingers across the cemetery.

"Fucking hell," I muttered. "The mausoleum has a supernatural leak."

The rot was spreading fast now, seeping into the grass, curling around tree roots, and creeping toward the other headstones.

Something deep in my gut twisted, and not just because I had downed that day-old banana muffin for breakfast.

Whatever was happening here, it was bad.

Like capital B, bolded, underlined <u>BAD</u>.

And somehow, it tied back to Grandpa Al.

My mostly fond memories of him—*the peppermint candies, the pineapple gifts, the always-too-strong cologne*—felt like they were about to get kicked in the metaphorical nuts.

Speaking of.

Time for a little magical clarity.

And I was hoping like hell since this had nothing to do with personal gain, that it worked.

I closed my eyes, steadied my breath, and chanted:

"In this hour,

I ask of thee,

Gaia of all powers that be,

That the sight increaseth in me,

Blood to blood, I call on family,

Today to see and nevermore,

Bring the ghost of Al Castor."

I waited. Worrying my bottom lip between my teeth.

My rhyming was objectively terrible, but I was

polite and I had passion—surely Gaia would count that for something?

I glanced down at my peach dress and matching sweater. The only reason I wasn't gagging more was because my cute little one-inch t-strap pumps were keeping my feet just above the thick puddles of magical snot collecting on the ground.

I really hoped they survived this encounter. Anthropologie wasn't cheap, and I had a budget to maintain.

Then, I heard it.

"Is that you, Evelyn?"

The voice boomed right in my ear.

I shrieked like a banshee and spun so fast my balance went bye-bye. I slipped, butt-first, into the slime with a sickening SPLURCH.

"Oh, come on!" I wheezed as green goo oozed into places it absolutely did not belong.

My stomach rolled.

The muffin? Officially regretted.

A deep chuckle rolled through the air.

Floating above the gravestones, with all the dramatic flair of a Vegas magician on acid, was my very dead grandfather.

And he was *pants less.*

Or—more accurately—he was see-through where most of his pants should have been.

And in place of, ahem, *manly bits*, was a giant red "NO" sign.

Like the Ghostbusters logo.

But just for Grandpa's, um, *junk*.

Oh my Goddess!

It all clicked into place.

The junkless wonder.

It was him. My dearly departed Grandpa Al!

"Evelyn, bellissima! Is that you?"

My eyes widened. My breathing increased.

"Uh, yeah, it's me," I murmured. "Um, hi, Grandpa. You, uh, look good. Except for the whole decaying and disembodied thing," I said, forcing a smile while discreetly trying to wipe goo off my ass.

He grinned wide, cigar ghost-flickering in his mouth, his massive square shades tinted brown like an old-timey mob accountant.

Dressed in the world's most offensive 1970s golf ensemble—*lime green shirt, banana-yellow and brown plaid pants (well only part of the pants were visible, just the belt loops, then nothing, and more ugliness from the knees down)*—he was the embodiment of every bad fashion choice ever made.

"You look just like your Nonna. A real knockout," he said proudly.

"Thanks, I think," I muttered, flicking a slime-glob off my shoulder.

"Is she here?" Grandpa Al asked, peering around. "That woman! Even dead, she drives me wild. She literally killed me, you know."

"Wait, WHAT?" I shouted, slipping again as my foot squished in a puddle. "Nonna killed you?"

"Well, technically, heart attack," he said with a shrug. "But what's a man supposed to do when the love of his life zaps his manhood to the Netherworld?"

I blinked. "She what?"

"Magically castrated me," he said, beaming. "One minute I was at poker night with the guys. Next, poof! No more *meatballs*."

My stomach did a full gymnastic routine.

"Grandpa, please stop talking."

"She caught me sleeping with her two best friends—*classic misunderstanding, really*—but boy, that temper! Loved that about her."

"You CHEATED! On Nonna?"

"Only a little," he said, crossing ghostly arms over his see-through crotch. "I had needs, Evelyn."

"You unbelievable son of a—"

A piercing howl cut through my outrage.

I looked up just in time to see a giant gray Wolf barreling toward me, teeth bared, followed by a mountain-sized Grizzly and a Python as thick as a water main.

"Holy fuck," I whispered, scrambling to my feet.

"Friends of yours?" Grandpa asked, tilting his head.

"Shut up, Grandpa!" I yelled.

The Wolf skidded to a stop, placing himself between me and the ghost, snarling like he was ready to eat the afterlife.

"Oh, for Gaia's sake," Grandpa sighed. "Who brings a dog to a séance?"

And that was the moment I knew this day was going to get even weirder.

CHAPTER TWENTY-FOUR-EVIE

"SHIFTERS? Are they new to Castor's Corner, Evie?" Grandpa Al tsked, floating in midair like he was judging our dinner menu and not the state of our supernatural security.

"You know what that means for our town," he said, as if I didn't freaking know.

"Shut up, you," I snapped, shooting him a glare that would've withered a living man's nethers—*if he still had any.*

"Evie!" Donny's shout rang through the fog, followed by Maribella huffing like she'd just run a marathon in stilettos.

They skidded to a halt beside me, cheeks flushed, eyes wide.

"We're here to help battle the—uh," Donny trailed

off mid-bravado, squinting up at the hovering, fashion-disaster ghost. "Wait. Isn't that your Grandpa?"

"Oh my goddess," Maribella wheezed. "He's real. And pantsless. Oh my gods, why is he pantsless?"

"Oh my!" Grandpa Al blinked, wiping spectral mist from his giant square glasses.

"How you've grown! Turn around, *ragazzi*, let me look at you!"

"What are you talking about, Grandpa?" I asked, trying very hard to ignore the way my dress was still soggy with goo. "You're acting like you know them."

He beamed like someone had just handed him a tray of cannoli.

"You girls! *My girls*! You've grown up so well."

Donny gave me a very suspicious side-eye. "Evie, the missing kids? It's the Fox twins—Ginger and Nugget."

My stomach dropped. "No. Not them."

The Fox twins were second graders—little, giggly, fuzzy-eared fox Shifters who always gave me dandelion bouquets and licked icing off bakery counters. The idea of them in danger?

Not. On. My. Watch.

"Evelyn?" Grandpa Al's voice turned cautious, but I wasn't having it.

Aqua-colored flames danced along my fingertips. My magic wasn't just awake—it was hungry.

I motioned for my friends to move behind me. Time to handle this.

"Look," I said, stepping forward, "I don't care what went down between you and Nonna. I'm not here to talk about your missing—bits—or magical midlife crises. I'm here because two children are missing."

He blinked. "Children?"

"The Fox children," I growled. "Where are they?"

A beat passed.

"The only missing children here are you three," he said, all misty-eyed and sentimental.

Cue my stomach dropping again—*this time from a completely different sort of horror.*

"Wait, what?" I asked, barely above a whisper.

"You girls," he said, arms spread wide in ghostly grandpa pride. "You're all mine. *My granddaughters.*"

"What in the name of Gaia's burned biscotti are you talking about?" I said, staggering.

My Wolf—*my gorgeous, ever-loyal Wolf*—pressed against my leg in a silent show of support.

On instinct, Donny and Bella stepped closer to me too.

The Bear hovered behind Donny like a grumpy

guardian angel, and the Python curled protectively at Bella's side like a living feather boa, *sans actual feathers*, with fangs.

"Evelyn, Maribella, Donatella," Grandpa Al said, glowing with pride. "Three parts of a single magical bloodline. My bloodline."

"Nope. Nope nope nope," Maribella muttered, face pale.

"We're related?" Donny gasped, eyes going wide.

"Yes," he said proudly. "You are my legacy. The Trifecta. The most powerful magical bond Castor's Corner has seen in generations. My girls."

"But that doesn't make sense!" I blurted. "Our moms—your daughters—weren't even close growing up."

"Well, yes, that's because I was a very busy man. Handsome, charming, a little irresponsible."

He shrugged. Freaking shrugged.

"Grandpa!" I screeched.

"What? It was the seventies. I made mistakes. I was also cursed by a very angry, very sexy Witch who banished me from the town and turned my boy parts into ghost confetti."

"Gross," Donny gagged.

"I'm gonna hurl," Bella added, face green.

"You think you're gonna hurl? He said he loved

Nonna and then cheated on her with her best friends," I growled, fire practically shooting out of my ears.

"I had needs," Grandpa Al protested.

"Get a hobby!" I snapped. "Knitting! Jigsaw puzzles! Celibacy!"

He floated backwards, hands raised in surrender.

"Look, I'm sorry, okay? I've had time to reflect. A lot of time. Turns out, getting magically neutered and exiled is a real perspective-shifter."

I was about to unload another magical fireball of judgment when his voice softened.

"But that wasn't the worst of it," he said. "Being away from Castor's Corner, from all of you? Now, that was the real punishment."

The words hit like a spell straight to the chest.

My fingers uncurled. Slowly.

"So why now?" I asked.

"Because the wards fell," he explained. "Just for a moment, a few days ago. And I slipped through. I've been haunting the cemetery, hoping one of you would show."

"I saw you," I whispered, realization dawning. "The night Jaxson and I met."

He raised a bushy ghost brow.

"You and the Wolf, huh? I thought I sensed a

claiming hovering in the air. Good instincts. Very primal. I like him."

"Focus!" Donny barked.

"Right, right. So, you have the sight, Evelyn. You can do more than just see the past. You can walk it."

I blinked. "You mean like *time travel?*"

"Kind of," he said. "More like spirit projection. It's not easy. But if you can tap into a powerful enough memory, you can visit it. Let it guide you."

Maribella gasped. "You're a true *Seer Witch*, Evie."

I closed my eyes and searched for the warmest memory I could find.

It came instantly.

I was three years old. On the beach.

My Nonna's kisses on my cheeks, my Grandpa lifting me onto his shoulders, sprinting along the waves while I shrieked in delight.

That memory flooded my senses—and for a moment, it was real.

The sea spray. The sun. The warmth.

When I opened my eyes, I was crying.

"That was incredible," I whispered.

"You're incredible," Grandpa Al said gently. "Now do you believe?"

I did.

And I had work to do.

"Grandpa, um, not to sound ungrateful, but what do you *want*?" I asked, knowing there had to be something else.

"To come home," he said. "My body was buried far away. Alone. Under fake names and shame. I want to be with family again. Please. Bring me back to the mausoleum."

"I'll think about it," I said carefully.

"Thank you, my girl," he said, already starting to fade.

"Wait!" I cried. "The kids—the Fox twins. Do you know where they are?"

He shook his head.

"I swear I don't. But if I find anything on the other side, I'll try to send you a sign."

And then he was gone.

And I had a problem.

A few of them, actually.

CHAPTER TWENTY-FIVE-EVIE

"YOU KNOW, we could always call Eric Smith. You know, with the Order of Witches? He can probably sniff out the kids and take out whoever took them, Donny whispered, clearly not wanting to deal with the reality of Grandpa Al's confession.

"Okay, let's put that on hold. There's just something about Eric Smith's blank eyes that makes me all *brrrrrrr*," Maribella said.

"What the heck does that mean?"

But she ignored the question, and she let out a long, slow breath.

"So, we're cousins. And Seers. And magic slime is probably soaking into my socks."

Donny nodded. "I want to barf. But also, that was kind of beautiful?"

"Let's go save those kids before I lose my mind," I muttered, wiping my cheeks. "And someone remind me to add 'exorcise Grandpa's junk ghost' to the to-do list."

"Got it," Maribella chirped. "Right under 'buy new shoes.'"

"Thanks," I sighed. "Gaia help us all."

And together, we turned toward the rot-filled shadows—ready to take on whatever came next.

Of course, that meant the Fates were cooking up a doozy.

But I didn't know it yet. I just turned to look at my two best friends—scratch that.

My actual, real-life cousins.

Bewildered and stunned were the two words that immediately came to mind, but something deeper clicked into place inside me.

Something ancient. Something true.

Without thinking, I launched myself at them, flinging my arms around both their necks and hugging them like my life depended on it.

"Holy Shitake Mushrooms," Maribella wheezed, squeezed between my boobs and Donny's curls.

"Can't breathe, but like, emotionally? Love this," Donny gasped.

Our magic responded instantly, pulsing and

flaring to life as if it had been waiting for this moment too.

Red. Aqua. Pink. Gold. Silver.

All our signature colors danced like fireworks in the gloomy graveyard, painting the shadows with light.

It felt like a hug from Gaia herself.

"Cousins?" Maribella said, voice wobbling between laughter and shock.

"Yeah," Donny breathed, swallowing hard.

"Cousins," I repeated, smiling so wide it hurt.

I couldn't help it. I'd loved them fiercely as my best friends.

But this? This changed everything.

This was blood and bones and shared legacy.

We were bound tighter than ever before, and the power of it hummed in the air like a symphony of old magic finally being played again.

Something flickered. An object. A shade? Oh—Grandpa Al?

He was back.

I released the girls and turned to face Grandpa Al, suddenly needing to thank him—*but his face had changed.*

He was staring past us, his translucent body flickering with panic.

"What is it, Grandpa?" I asked, stepping forward.

His eyes locked on mine. "Evelyn! I-I came back to warn you. All of you! There is danger! You must go! Go! Now!"

I didn't have time to ask what he meant before a low, ominous roar tore through the sky.

We all turned. A massive funnel cloud was barreling toward the cemetery, twisting unnaturally through the trees.

This wasn't your average weather anomaly.

No way.

This was something else.

The winds shrieked, tearing up earth and tombstones as they spiraled.

The ghost of Grandpa Al let out a cry as the vortex latched onto him—*pulling him ghost-feet first toward the howling mouth of the storm.*

"Run! Go now! Run, ragazzi! Be saaaaaaaffffe!" he shouted as he was sucked up into the dark spiral and vanished in a swirl of mist and magic.

My heart clenched, but there was no time to mourn.

The Shifters didn't need another warning.

The Bear roared. The Python hissed. And my Wolf—my glorious, smoldering, pain-in-the-ass-soon-to-be-mate—let out a low yip and bounded to my side.

Get on, Evie. Jaxson's voice echoed in my mind, calm and fierce. *We have to leave. Now.*

I blinked. "Oh, fuck," Donny swore. "You guys heard that, right? The telepathy thing? That's real?"

Maribella looked equally shocked.

"We're mentally connected to magical man meat?! This is either the best or worst day of my life!"

I grinned despite the chaos, grabbing both their hands one last time.

"We'll unpack the brain-sex later, ladies. Ride now. Bonded brainwaves later."

I threw a leg over my Wolf's broad, furry back, and he took off like a rocket.

His fur tickled my thighs, and I wrapped my arms around his neck, gripping tight as he zigzagged through the storm-tossed cemetery like he'd been born for this moment.

Maybe he had.

Behind me, I saw Donny clinging to the hulking bear Shifter, her wild curls streaming like a banner of defiance.

Bella was coiled around the snake, her fingers

knotted in his smooth, scaly bulk like she was riding a giant magical jungle gym.

"THIS IS FINE!" Bella screamed, clearly not fine.

Then I looked back.

And my stomach dropped.

The funnel cloud was no ordinary weather tantrum. Deep inside the swirling mass, eyes glowed.

Red ones.

Malevolent and alive.

"Oh Gaia," I breathed. "That's no storm. That's a fucking entity."

And that's when it hit me—*if we fled, what was stopping that thing from following us straight into town? To the children? To the people of Castor's Corner?*

No way.

"STOP!" I shouted, yanking on Jaxson's fur like it was a parking brake. "Stop, we can't run from this!"

He skidded to a halt, his body jerking slightly from the force of it. I nearly toppled off, but before I could even curse, there was a shimmer, a shift, and suddenly I was cradled in his arms.

His very naked arms.

"Goddess, really?" I grumbled, waving my hand instinctively.

A shimmer of peach magic clothed him in jeans and a T-shirt just in time.

Because naked Jaxson mid-storm?

That was a dangerous distraction I did not have time for. Plus, I couldn't say I would be happy if anyone else ogled him.

His lips curved in that cocky way that made me want to kiss and slap him all at once.

"What? I thought you liked the full moon."

"Not now, Wolf," I muttered, pressing a palm against his chest. "That thing? It's not just a storm. It's sentient."

"What do we do?" he asked, serious again.

I looked back toward the whirling vortex, its red eyes flashing, hungry and full of wrath.

My magic tingled in my veins, the weight of our Trifecta legacy humming inside me.

"We make a stand," I said, meeting my mate's eyes. "Together."

He nodded once. "Then let's show this town what its mayor—*and her magical mafia of cousins*—can do."

The winds howled louder, as if accepting our challenge.

And I stood tall, heart pounding, magic rising, and whispered, "Let's give this storm something to fear."

CHAPTER TWENTY-SIX-
JAXSON

I SQUINTED at the swirling black cloud twisting above us like a pissed-off god had dropped his laundry and decided to weaponize it.

The red eyes lurking within glowed hotter, hungrier. I felt Evie step forward before I saw it—and not just with my eyes.

I have to do this.

Her voice wasn't spoken.

It echoed in my mind like a whisper in the dark, warm and brave and stubborn as hell.

"Evelyn?" I called out, worry sharpening my voice as the wind tore around us, flinging leaves like they were shrapnel.

"I have to do this," she shouted back aloud, steady against the chaos.

The leaves spiraled, the air crackled, but she didn't flinch.

My mate—*my mate, even if I hadn't sunk my teeth into her yet*—stood at the heart of the storm like she was the storm.

Donny and Maribella rushed to her side.

"We want to help!" Donny called out, her golden curls whipping like streamers.

"No! It's too dangerous," Evie warned.

"Hush up now, Madam Mayor!" Bella snapped, already taking her place beside her. "You just focus and do your thing, 'cause we aren't going anywhere."

The two Witches stood shoulder to shoulder with her, hips cocked, ready for war in the cemetery like it was just another Saturday.

I stayed quiet.

Watching. Waiting.

Holding back the urge to run to her and yank her behind me.

That would've been easier—safer.

But it would've insulted the fire I saw in her eyes.

And the truth was, I trusted her. More than anyone.

He trusts me to do this. All of them do.

No one's ever put that kind of trust in me before.

I heard that too.

Every word, raw and reverberating through our matebond like she'd carved them into my chest.

I didn't choose to be mayor, she continued, *but it's my destiny. Just like he is.*

My breath caught.

I'm going to mate the big Wolf man the second this is over.

A growl nearly escaped me, low and possessive and mine, but I held it in.

Barely.

Gaia help me, I was going to make her keep that promise.

First things first. I have some kids to save. And some windy-ass to kick.

Oh, fuck me—I loved her.

She stepped forward, chin raised high, power snapping around her like the air before a lightning strike.

Her magic shimmered like aquamarine fire around her shoulders.

"Hey, Shit Storm!" she yelled at the funnel cloud. "You took our kids, and I want them back!"

The tornado spasmed mid-air like a broken-down engine about to die.

Then it *morphed*.

I blinked.

It grew arms and legs.

It stomped toward us in a shiny-ass sharkskin suit so tight I could count the number of veins on its tiny little prick.

"Gaia's tits," I muttered as Evie's overactive gag reflex gagged loudly enough for all of us to hear.

"Fuck, fuck, fuck!" the thing screeched—*and then I realized it wasn't a thing.*

It really was a prick. As in Dick.

Dick Daniels.

Somehow, the most annoying Wizard in town had transformed into the human equivalent of mildew and ego with an actual face.

He waved his wand and used magic to expand his clothing.

Thank Gaia.

"Too bad he can't use that spell to make his ding-a-ling bigger," Donny snorted under her breath.

"Shh!" Bella hissed—but I saw the corners of her mouth twitch.

I was this close to laughing too, but Evie's sharp gasp snapped me back to focus.

I followed her line of sight.

There. Two little Red Fox Shifter kids.

Bound and caged like goddamn pets. Rage surged inside me.

Hell no.

A low snarl built in my throat. My Wolf was ready to rip and tear.

"That's better," Dick said, dusting off his stupid suit. "Now, Evelyn, removing me as Fire Chief was not your brightest move—but you're just a woman. We all know a man would be a better fit as mayor of Castor's Corner."

My fists clenched.

I stepped forward, but Evie raised a hand—*not yet.*

"I was even thinking a name change," Dick continued. "We could call it Daniels' Square."

"Dick, what the ever-living fuck are you talking about?" Evie growled.

I nearly cheered. That was my girl.

My fingers are itching to zap this asshole into next week. Can I do that? I'm a Seer Witch. I have no fucking idea what I can do, but I'm willing to try, Evie's voice sounded in my head.

Oh yes, please, I wanted to shout.

Dick went on with his monologue of douchebaggery.

"I'm talking about the mistake I made wasting

time trying to date you. I should've just done this back then."

"Done what exactly?" she demanded.

Ignore the growl. Oh, but I really do like when he gets possessive. Super turn-on. We will talk about my Wolf-man's sexy growls later—focus.

I choked.

But inside? I agreed.

We were definitely talking about that later.

Also later, I was going to show my Witchy mate just how much I liked her, too.

I was going to find everyone of her pleasure buttons, and I was going to *press press press* away.

Dick sneered.

"Do I have to spell it out? I'm going to kill these mongrels unless you step down. Castor's Corner is a joke! A town for Witches and Wizards only. Your family polluted it by letting everyone in. Now, I'm taking over—and I'm going to clean up."

"You know what, Dick?" Evie raised her hands, her magic coiling like a tidal wave behind her. "I don't fucking think so."

Her aura exploded, blinding aqua light blazing as her hair lifted on the wind and her eyes glowed with Seer fire.

The storm paused.

So did my heartbeat.

She was a vision. A goddess. My mate.

And Castor's Corner had no idea how lucky it was to have her.

But that bastard Wizard was about to find out.

CHAPTER TWENTY-SEVEN- EVIE

POWER PULSED through me like never before.

I was so damn mad at Dick.

How dare he come to my town, date me, dump me, kidnap Mrs. Fox's children, and now, he was making plans for an all-out banishment of supernaturals who weren't Witch or Wizard?

Hell. No.

I raised my hand.

Aqua flames shot from my fingertips, wrapping around the now-screaming Wizard like a magical Python of justice.

Dick Daniels writhed on the ground, flopping and screeching like a fish in a deep fryer.

But I didn't let up.

"Get the children!" I yelled, even though I knew I didn't need to.

Jaxson and his buddies were already moving, a blur of fur and fangs turned muscle and grit as they charged toward the cage holding the terrified Fox twins.

Donny and Bella raced beside them, hands glowing as they zapped through the magical locks like seasoned pros.

"You thought you could shame me? Trick me? Blackmail me into handing over this town?" I spat, keeping the heat of my magic focused.

Dick shrieked like a banshee in a discount business suit. "You never even wanted Castor's Corner, Evie! You said that on our first date, remember? You called it a burden!"

"Oh, I *remember*," I said with a snarl. "But I changed my damn mind. Castor's Corner isn't a burden. It's my *destiny*. And as long as I'm mayor, I will protect it with every spark in my soul."

"I just wanted to clean up this town!" he howled, flailing dramatically as if he were starring in some off-Broadway supernatural soap.

"No, Dick. You're just a power-hungry asshat. And the *only* thing we need to clean up around here is *you*."

My knees buckled slightly.

Holding his writhing, snotty self in place with raw magic was draining every bit of juice I had left—*but I wasn't alone.*

Bella and Donny stepped in, power flaring in gold and pink, their hands lifting as they took the magical reins.

"Thanks, cousins," I whispered with a tired grin. They winked, then nodded for me to do what I had to do.

I took a breath, felt the magic gather deep in my core, then launched into the spell.

A little ancient, a little improvised, and very much from the heart.

"Gaia on high,
Hear my call,
This racist fucker
Must answer to all.
For his crimes against
Our children and more,
We cast Dick Daniels
Far from our shore.
Across time and space,
I ask you to send
This tiny-pricked ass
To a place without friends."

And with that, I summoned the great shimmering ball of aqua-colored power I'd been holding inside and flung it at him like a fast-pitch softball of doom.

The explosion lit up the cemetery.

When the dust settled, all that remained of Dick was a blackened scorch mark on the grass and a faint scent of cheap aftershave.

"Shit, I'm tired," I gasped—*and the world tilted sideways.*

Strong arms caught me before I face-planted into the grass.

"Easy," Jaxson murmured, his voice warm and rough at my ear as he scooped me up like I weighed nothing. "I got you, darlin'."

"You sure do, Wolfman," I mumbled. "If you want me?"

He blinked down at me like I'd just handed him the moon.

"Are you serious?"

"Uh-huh," I whispered. "I want you to mate me, Jaxson. For real. I want to wear your claiming bite. I want you to stay in Castor's Corner. With me."

"And my friends?" he asked, glancing at the other two.

Conrad and Ryan, now in their human forms, were watching with cautious hope in their eyes.

Bella and a flushed Donny stood nearby, cradling the rescued Fox twins.

"Well, I'm a one-Wolf kinda Witch," I said, teasing him.

"Damn fucking straight you are. I meant, can they stay?"

Jaxson narrowed his lightning-bright eyes at me, and mock-frowned, but his teasing grin told me he was more than a match for my sass.

"Well, I believe Castor's Corner is looking for a fire crew, and it seems we just got a new sheriff," I said with a tired smile. "Think you three are up for it long term?"

"Yes, ma'am," Conrad and Ryan chorused.

"Good," I managed. "Now, Jaxson?"

"What is it, Darlin'?"

"Take me home, I think I'm gonna—"

And just like that, I passed the hell out.

CHAPTER TWENTY-EIGHT-EVIE

I WOKE UP HOURS LATER, tucked safely into my bed and—*yep*—totally naked.

Honestly, that was probably for the best.

I wouldn't want to get magical ooze on my favorite floral sheets.

"You alive?" a gruff voice asked.

I groaned and peeked open one eye. "Ivan?"

The Domovyk sat at the foot of my bed like a squat little judgmental gargoyle with a permanent scowl.

"Yeah. No thanks to you. I thought you were my familiar, aren't you supposed to help me?" I growled, clutching the blanket to my chest.

I always thought familiars were supposed to *assist* Witches with their magic—ya know, so we didn't keel over from magical burnout.

And maybe, *just maybe,* show up when we're facing down psychotic Wizard ex-boyfriends.

"I helped," he huffed. "I got your Grandpa Al back. And I cleaned the cemetery. Magical ooze removal. You're welcome."

"What slime?"

"You didn't *notice* the green goo dripping all over your family mausoleum?" Ivan asked, eyes bugging slightly.

"Oh, *that* slime. Ew. Why was it there?"

"It was a curse. The Wizard wanted your position and your power. Weak curses leave behind residue. Sticky residue. Very bad for property value."

"Wait. How did you clean it? You're like four feet tall."

"Excuse you, I am four feet two and one third inches," he scoffed. "I am also an expert in banishment rituals. And I borrowed your vacuum."

"You used my thousand-dollar Witch-Shark Vac on demon goo?"

"It was very effective."

I slapped my hand over my face. "Gaia help me."

"I already did," Ivan said smugly. "Also, you didn't see me at the fight?"

"Uh, no?"

"I was there. Invisible, of course. Got your backside."

"You mean *you had my back*," I corrected.

"No. I mean your actual backside. Those sheets were a tragedy."

"Typical male," I muttered.

He stood up with a grumble. "Your Grandpa Al is safe. But he needs a proper burial. The tornado flung him all the way to Barvale. I brought him back."

"Wait—Barvale?" I sat up too fast and instantly regretted it. "Holy hell. You brought him back?"

"Of course. I do my job. Also, your Werewolf is in the kitchen making stew. I will require two bowls. And some of those garlic knots he bought."

"Stew?" I blinked.

"Yes. He cooks. And you passed out. He has been pacing like a lunatic and muttering about magical exhaustion and 'damn stubborn Witches.'" Ivan narrowed his eyes. "He's a keeper. Do not screw it up."

"Thanks, Ivan," I said, genuinely touched.

"You are welcome," he grunted. "Now I go before you try to kiss me."

And with a pop, he vanished from the bed.

I blinked, dazed, smiling stupidly at the ceiling.

My familiar believed in me.

My Grandpa's ghost had my back.

My best friends were my cousins.

My town was safe.

And downstairs, my fated mate was making me *stew*.

For once in my life, everything felt *right*.

Even if I was still naked and had a little dried ghost goo on my skin.

CHAPTER TWENTY-NINE- JAXSON

I WAS JUST LADLING out the second bowl of stew—*mama's recipe, slow-cooked with love and enough garlic to scare off a whole nest of Vamps*—when I heard it.

Soft footsteps. A breath too careful.

If I didn't have supernatural hearing, I might've missed the tiptoe creak of her coming down the stairs.

But I did. And more than that, I could *smell* her.

That warm, sweet, citrus-vanilla blend that always hits me low and hard. Wildflowers, magic, and pure lust.

Evie. My Evie.

I turned, bowl still in hand, and nearly dropped the damn thing.

There she was, padding into the kitchen like temptation incarnate—barefoot, tousled, and wearing a pajama set that was doing something unholy to my restraint.

The soft shorts barely covered that thick, plush ass I wanted to bite, and the long-sleeved tee clung to curves that made my mouth go dry.

"Hey," she said, voice soft but steady.

That one word lit up every nerve ending in my body.

"Hey," I croaked out like a fool.

That was all I could manage.

Every damn time I laid eyes on this woman, I turned into a tongue-tied idiot.

A six-foot-six, Alpha-dominant Werewolf with the communication skills of a sock.

"You hungry?" I asked, gesturing with the bowl before setting it on the table.

She gave me a wicked grin. "Always, Wolfman."

I barked a laugh—*couldn't help it*—and set both bowls down before walking to her.

I didn't ask.

I just reached for her hand and pulled her against my chest, wrapping her up in a hug that felt like home.

She melted into me like we'd done this every day of our lives.

"Thank you, Jaxson," she whispered, her cheek pressed against my chest. I felt the words more than heard them.

"For what, Darlin'?"

"For being here. For taking care of me. For believing in me when I wasn't sure I could believe in myself."

"Evelyn Castor, I will *always* be here for you."

She tipped her head back and looked at me, and what I saw in those whiskey-brown eyes just about leveled me.

Vulnerability. Hope. Maybe even love.

"Do you mean that?" she asked quietly. "And do you still want to mate me?"

My heart squeezed so hard I had to breathe through it.

I cupped her face gently, rubbed my thumbs along the apples of her cheeks.

"More than I want air. I love you, Evie Castor," I confessed.

"You do? Because, um, I love you too, Jaxson Reid."

I wanted to throw my head back and howl to the whole damn world. She loved me. And everything was better for it.

"Dammit, Evie, the things I want to do to you," I growled and nipped her earlobe between my teeth, and she damn near swooned.

"Yes, please."

"Oh, I will, Darlin'. But all the delicious things I plan on doing to you tonight? They require strength. Stamina. *Hydration.* So here's the plan."

Her lips parted, eyes wide, body leaning into mine like she already knew what I was going to say.

"You're gonna sit your sweet ass in my lap, let me feed you every last bite of this stew," I said, voice low and rough, "then I'm carrying you upstairs. And I'm gonna fuck you right. *Claim* you deep. Make sure you never doubt who you belong to."

Her breath hitched, and my own control frayed like an old rope.

"Because I already know, one hundred percent—Evie Castor, I belong to *you.*"

She made a soft sound in her throat that had me half-hard instantly.

I pulled out a chair and sat, patting my lap. She didn't hesitate.

Just climbed on, curling against me like she'd been born there.

And I fed her.

Bite by bite.

Perfectly tender beef, buttery carrots, soft peas, and the best damn broth you ever tasted.

Her eyes fluttered closed every time I brought the spoon to her lips, like she was savoring more than just food.

After the last bite, I wiped her lips with my thumb and kissed her, slow and lingering, before standing with her still in my arms.

She gasped and wrapped her arms around my neck.

"You're really carrying me upstairs? I'm too heavy—"

I cut off that line of nonsense with a swat to her sweet ass.

"Darlin', I told you already. Strength and endurance." I grinned and kissed her nose. "I got both. And for the record, you're not too heavy. You're fucking perfect."

By the time I kicked the bedroom door open, she was already tugging at my shirt like it offended her.

I tossed her onto the bed and followed right after, crawling over her, nosing at her neck, taking in her scent like a starving man.

She arched for me—legs open, body ready, eyes wild with want.

"Clothes," she panted. "Off. Now."

"Yes, ma'am." I made quick work of them both.

My shirt hit the wall.

Her top hit the lamp.

I didn't even remember how her shorts came off, but they were gone, and she was spread out like a feast.

Gaia help me, she was so *wet*, so ready.

"Need you inside me, Jaxson," she begged, pulling at me. "Now. No teasing."

That voice?

That sweet, commanding need?

It flipped some kind of primal switch in me.

My Wolf howled inside, clawing to claim.

I lined up and pushed in deep with a guttural growl.

Her gasp punched straight into my soul.

"Fuuuck," I hissed, barely holding on as her heat gripped me, tight and perfect and mine.

She was everything.

Soft and fierce. Sweet and sinful.

And she was *mine.*

I drove into her hard and deep, setting a pace that had her eyes rolling back and her hips lifting to meet me.

Her fingers scratched down my back, her mouth chanting my name like a prayer and a curse.

Every stroke, every slide, pulled a broken sound from her throat—*and I ate them up like candy.*

Her magic flared—blue and red and silver and wild.

It sparked along my skin like fireflies made of power.

The bond between us *snapped* taut, and I felt her—*really felt her*—body and soul.

"I'm close," she whimpered. "Jaxson, I—oh Gaia—"

"I've got you, Darlin'. Come for me. Let me *have* you."

Her walls clenched, a cry ripped from her throat—and that's when I *bit.*

I sank my fangs deep into the slope of her neck, right over the thrumming pulse that screamed *mine.*

Her climax exploded.

Her back bowed, legs shaking as her power surged around us in a blinding wave of aqua flame.

I followed her over the edge, roaring her name as I came, grinding deep as I spilled inside her.

Our *matebond* sealed with a rush of magic and heat and pure, unrelenting *rightness.*

She was mine.

I was hers.

Forever.

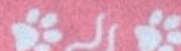

EPILOGUE-EVIE

EVIE–CASTOR'S **Corner, Present Day**

"For fuck's sake!" I groaned as my laptop pinged for what felt like the *eleventh* time.

Three days.

That's how long I'd been tangled up in bedsheets with one very attentive Wolf Shifter.

Three glorious days of being thoroughly loved, kissed, claimed, and, let's be honest, thoroughly ruined in the best possible way.

Jaxson called it our honeymoon—even if we weren't "married" in the human sense.

But we weren't human.

Not even close.

I was a Witch. A *Seer*, to be exact. And he?

He was my mate. A Wolf Shifter who smelled like

lemon and basil and made me feel like the most precious thing on this planet.

Matings weren't just for now.

They were *forever*.

And I'd never felt more safe, more wanted, or more *mine*.

Stanley was covering things at Town Hall until I returned later this afternoon, but apparently, someone missed the memo that the mayor was off-duty for magical mating reasons.

The nerve.

"What is that sound?" Jaxson called from the kitchen, his deep voice dripping with sleepy heat.

"It's Swoosh," I grumbled, grabbing a robe and trying to sound annoyed instead of completely blissed out.

"S'what?" he teased, padding barefoot into view with nothing but a low-slung pair of gray sweatpants and a smirk that could melt my panties off.

"Not S'what, *Swoosh*—our messaging system." I waved vaguely toward the laptop. "Don't worry about it."

"Mmm, don't go," he growled, appearing behind me in an instant to nip at the curve of my neck.

My knees went weak. His spicy little love bite zinged straight to my core. I bit back a moan.

Gaia help me, maybe I *should* stay in bed. The man made a strong case.

Ping.

Damn it.

"I'm sorry," I sighed, but he was already kissing me senseless again.

When he finally pulled away, I could barely remember what day it was.

"You never have to apologize to me, Darlin'," he said with a crooked grin, brushing a strand of hair behind my ear. "You answer that, and I'll wrangle us up some breakfast."

"'Kay," I whispered, already missing his warmth.

"With blueberries?" he called over his shoulder.

I froze, blinking.

"You heard that?"

He chuckled low in his throat. "Matebond, remember? You think it, I feel it. Very handy when I'm trying to blow your mind in bed."

"Gaia help me," I muttered, blushing furiously.

"Love you back, Darlin'," he added, and just like that, my heart did a happy little cartwheel.

Turning back to my still-barking laptop, I opened the invitation to join the video chat with a sigh.

"OMG, EVELYN! HE DID IT AGAIN! LOOK! POOP IN ALL MY SHOES!"

Donny's furious face filled the screen, cheeks flushed, hair in curlers, waving what looked like a ballet flat full of Domovyk doo.

I snorted, nearly falling off my chair.

Gryn, her snippy little familiar, was clearly on a mission to make her life hell.

Now, we'd each been gifted a Domovyk by La Befana herself, the most powerful Witch working in North America under the Morrigan.

And I didn't dare complain.

Ivan—*my Domovyk familiar*—was actually growing on me.

Like a magically grumpy fungus.

Bella seemed fine with Petyr.

Only Donny wasn't quite getting the hang of life with Gryn.

Despite the hiccups, life in Castor's Corner was surprisingly good.

I was still mayor, and maybe for the first time, I wasn't resenting that title.

Stanley was back for good and officially off vacation.

Bella and Donny—*my besties, turned cousins, always magical ride-or-dies*—were thriving—*poopy shoe thing aside.*

The Fox twins were safe and sound.

And those three delicious Shifters?

They were now our new Castor's Corner Fire Department and the town's new Sheriff.

Oh, and my truck was finally fixed.

Thanks, Jeff.

Also? I had a mate. A fated mate.

My fated mate.

Jaxson.

Just thinking his name made my skin tingle and my magic spark.

The matebond between us was still new and electric, and every time I closed my eyes, I could feel it humming along my skin like a second heartbeat.

Goddess, how I loved that Wolfman.

Out of the blue, a cool fall breeze drifted through the window. My aqua-colored magic flared at my fingertips.

For a moment, I thought of Nonna and Grandpa Al.

I was moving forward with getting his remains back to our mausoleum.

I'd even called my parents and told them *everything.*

About the magic.

About Bella and Donny being my first cousins.

About Jaxson.

About how happy I finally was.

They cried. *Happy tears.*

And Jaxson?

He was always there when I called them. Shirtless. Holding a spatula. Mom *loved* him.

Snort.

Now, the town still had its moments—*suspicion about the new Shifter residents, the usual magical mishaps*—but I wasn't worried.

Because I wasn't facing any of it alone anymore.

I had my Wolf.

I had my cousins.

I had magic.

And for the first time in a long time, I was more than just okay with staying in Castor's Corner.

This place? These people? They were mine. And I was theirs.

Yes, I was home.

And I planned on staying and doing my best for the town. For my mate. For my friends and family.

Every. Single. Day.

The End... for now.

Did you enjoy this book? Awesome! Kindly leave a review so other readers might try it. I appreciate you so much! Now, are you hungry for more growly Shifters and wonderful Witches?

Check out the entire Hungry Fur Love series today! Just go here: https://www.cdgorri.com/series/hungry-fur-love

ALSO BY C.D. GORRI

<hr>

<u>Paranormal Romance Books by Series</u>

A Howlin' Good Fairytale Retelling

Barvale Holiday Tales

Dire Wolf Mates

Hearts of Stone Series

Hungry Fur Love

Island Stripe Pride

Jersey Sure Shifters/EveL Worlds

Lords of Nightfall

Macconwood Pack Novel Series

Macconwood Pack Tales Series

Mated in Hope Falls

Moongate Island Tales

Motley Crewd Shifters

NYC Shifter Tales

Purely Paranormal Romance Books

Speed Dating with the Denizens of the Underworld

The Barvale Clan Tales

The Bear Claw Tales

The Falk Clan Tales

The Guardians of Chaos

The Maverick Pride Tales

The Wardens of Terra

Twice Mated Tales

When Worlds Collide

Witch Shifter Clan

Wyvern Protection Unit

Young Adult/Urban Fantasy Books by Series

Blackthorn Academy For Supernaturals

G'Witches Magical Mysteries Series
Co-written with P. Mattern

The Angela Tanner Files

The Grazi Kelly Novel Series

Witches of Westwood Academy

with Gina Kincade

Contemporary Romance Books by Series & Title

Carolina Rugby Romance

A Reason To Try

The Break Down

A Game of Ruck

Dump Tackle My Heart

Support Your Local Hooker

Sin Bin for the Billionaire

Cherry On Top Tales

Her Yule His Log

His Carrot Her Muffin

Her Chocolate His Bar

His Pickle Her Jam

Her Trick His Treat

His Wood Her Fire

Her Birthday His Package

Jersey Bad Boys

Merciful Lies

Devious Lies

Pitiful Lies

Mergers & Acquisitions

Desperate Measures

Desperate Needs

Desperate Desires

Desperate Actions

Desperate People

Desperate Crimes

Desperate Games

Desperate Secrets

Wild Billionaire Romance

His Wild Obsession

His Wild Temptation

His Wild Seduction

His Wild Attraction

Bonus Scene His Wild Halloween Night

Wrecked Rockstar Romance

Dirty Lyrics

Broken Chords

Wicked Beats

Be sure to check out my BUY DIRECT BUNDLES and get 30% off when you buy available only my website.

Click here for The Official C.D. Gorri Reading List - free download

ABOUT THE AUTHOR

USA Today Bestselling Author C.D. Gorri writes steamy Paranormal & Contemporary Romance and Urban Fantasy packed with heart, humor, and heat.

Join her mailing list here: https://www.cdgorri.com/newsletter

A lifelong book lover, she's rarely without a story in hand, and her own tales reflect that passion. Based in her beloved New Jersey, C.D. weaves the Garden State into many of her stories, grounding even the wildest supernatural adventures with a touch of home.

Her books are fast-paced, full of feels, and always end with a satisfying HEA. You'll meet sassy, curvy heroines and the possessive, love-driven heroes who adore them, whether they're Shifters, Vampires,

Witches, or just morally gray men falling hard in her contemporary worlds.

If you're into fated mates, fierce love, and action-packed romance where loyalty wins and love always triumphs then *welcome*. You're in the right place.

Thanks for reading!

Del mare alla stella,

C.D. Gorri

Curvy Heroines & Epic Heroes for the avid reader.
http://www.cdgorri.com
https://www.facebook.com/Cdgorribooks
https://www.bookbub.com/authors/c-d-gorri
https://twitter.com/cgor22
https://instagram.com/cdgorri/
https://www.goodreads.com/cdgorri
https://www.tiktok.com/@cdgorriauthor